FALLEN ANGEL

HER ANGEL: BOUND WARRIORS
BOOK 2

FELICITY HEATON

First printed November 2018

Second Edition

Originally published as Her Fallen Angel in 2010

Layout and design by Felicity Heaton

THE HER ANGEL WORLD

HER ANGEL: BOUND WARRIORS

HER ANGEL: ETERNAL WARRIORS

Discover more available paranormal romance books at:
http://www.felicityheaton.com

Or sign up to my mailing list to receive a FREE vampire romance ebook, learn about new titles, be eligible for special subscriber-only giveaways, and read exclusive content including short stories:
http://ml.felicityheaton.com/mailinglist

CHAPTER 1

Lukas was looking worse for wear.

Annelie had never seen him drink alcohol. She had often wondered why he came to her pub but stuck to soft drinks. Seeing him slowly sliding down towards the wooden bar, his head propped up on his hand and his eyes closed, she was no longer surprised that he lay off the booze.

He couldn't handle it.

His scruffy sandy locks fell forwards when his head slipped from his hand and he jerked up.

He rolled his eyes a few times while blinking and then pulled a face as he inspected the damp elbow of his black shirt and the wet bar where he had been leaning.

A sigh lifted his broad shoulders and his green eyes shifted to the half-full glass of whisky in front of him, growing a little unfocused as he stared at it. He turned it on the bar, canting his head to his left as he studied it. The soft lighting above him reflected off the glass, casting patterns over the dark wood, and his gaze went from unfocused to hazy. Either he was lost in thought, or the whisky was really taking its toll on him.

Perhaps she should have cut him off after his third, but his charming smile had persuaded her to supply him with a fourth, and a fifth. She regretted it now, her stomach squirming whenever she looked at him and saw the effect of the alcohol on him.

At the time, he had looked as though he would be fine.

Now, he looked as though he was going to pass out.

Heck, maybe she shouldn't have given him the first shot.

What if he didn't drink because he was an alcoholic and she had just ruined his recovery?

She would never be able to live with herself if that was the case.

She handed some change to a patron and walked along the length of the area behind the bar to Lukas, neatening her appearance as she did so, a nervous habit she couldn't quite get under control whenever she was heading in his direction.

Her heart rate jacked up as she tugged the hem of her black baby-doll t-shirt down to sit smoothly along the waist of her black jeans and combed her fingers through her long red hair. She always felt as though she looked like a mess whenever things got frantic behind the bar.

And she wanted to look her best for Lukas.

She had been deeply aware of her appearance from the moment she had first set eyes on him, felt self-conscious whenever his eyes landed on her, and ached for them to return to her whenever he looked away.

Did he know how badly he affected her?

Did she affect him at all?

Her pulse raced faster and she struggled to breathe evenly as she neared him. They must have talked for hours in the years they had known each other, had shared secrets and laughs about all manner of things, but she still had to drag her courage up from her toes whenever she wanted to speak with him.

She nodded when an elderly man wished her a good night, offering him a warm smile that came straight from her heart. She had known him since she was a kid, back when her parents had run the old bar that was now hers and she had been more interested in running around and talking to all the regulars, showing them her latest paintings or hearing their stories.

Annelie glanced around to make sure that no one needed her.

The pub was quieter now that it was approaching closing time. A few regulars remained along with a group of people she didn't recognise who were sitting in the corner near the bay windows that overlooked the road.

She could finally speak to Lukas without interruption.

She sucked down a quiet breath.

Leaned on the damp bar opposite Lukas, between two sets of pumps.

Reached a trembling hand out and swept his fair hair out of his eyes.

He leaned away, almost fell off his stool, clutched the brass rail that ran around the edge of the bar to stop himself, and then looked at her.

An all-too-familiar jolt shot through her when his clear green eyes met her brown ones and her heart fluttered in her chest when he smiled lopsidedly.

"You okay?" She went to take her hand away but he took hold of it, bringing it down to the bar.

She swallowed hard as he toyed with her fingers, his warm and firm against them, and her heart thundered, hammering against her chest as her mouth dried out.

His gaze fell to their joined hands, a flicker of fascination entering his eyes, and she told herself not to read into it.

So what if this was the first bordering-on-intimate contact they'd had?

So what if he had made her heart stop the moment he had first walked into her pub three years ago and it had stopped every time she had seen him since?

It didn't mean anything.

At least, it didn't mean anything to him.

Sure, they had talked and whiled away the hours, and Lukas was an amazing listener and always seemed genuinely interested in her problems and helping her solve them, but he had never once shown any interest in her beyond friendship.

She wished that he would.

He was drop dead gorgeous. Six feet plus of masculine beauty. And she wanted to pounce on him whenever he walked through the door.

Which had been almost every other night until recently.

He had gone away for three long weeks without a word, leaving her wondering if something terrible had happened to him.

And then the moment he walked back into her life, he hit the drink.

Hard.

Lukas didn't answer her. His green gaze remained fixed on her hand and he turned it this way and that, his touch gentle now. Her heart whispered that this was interest beyond friendship. She tried to shut it up but it persisted, filled her head with the ridiculous thought that she might finally get her wish, that those dreams she had of Lukas were finally going to become real.

Annelie shut it down, because disappointment and heartache lay down that road.

Lukas was just drunk, tired and, by the looks of things, a little out of sorts. For the first time, he looked as if he was the one who needed to unburden his shoulders and his heart, and she was determined to listen to him as he had listened to her so many times in the past. She was going to help him. It was the least she could do for him.

Someone stepped up to the bar at the far end and she waved to Andy to serve him. She couldn't leave Lukas until she knew what was going on in his head and why he was suddenly drinking, or at least until she was sure he wasn't about to fall off his stool and hurt himself.

Annelie bent lower so she could see his face.

His gaze finally left her hand and met hers again, bright in the lights from the mirrored cabinet of bottles behind her.

"I said you okay?" She searched his eyes.

His pupils were wide as he raked his gaze down over her chest, fire following in its wake, and then lifted it back up to her face. It remained fixed there and a blush crept onto her cheeks as he studied her, the intensity and sudden sharpness of his eyes holding her captive even when she wanted to glance away and avoid his gaze. He had never looked at her so closely, or with so much banked heat in his eyes.

Heat that rippled through her and had her deeply aware of the way his hand held hers and how close she was to him.

"Hell of a week." His reply was so quiet that she barely heard him.

"You've been gone three." Those words slipped from her lips before she could stop them, laced with hurt that surprised her, had her reeling a little as she stared at him and felt the heavy press of that pain on her heart.

She had thought she had been worried about Lukas when he had disappeared on her, but now she realised it had hurt her too. She had been afraid she would never see him again.

4

His eyebrows rose. "Three?"

Annelie nodded. Lukas released her hand and she mourned the loss of contact, ached for him to touch her again, to hold her because it had been reassuring her that he was back with her now.

He heaved a long sigh and ran his hand over the messy finger-length strands of his hair, preening it back, before pinching the bridge of his nose. His eyes screwed shut.

"Hell of a three weeks." Lukas smiled but she saw straight through it.

Something was wrong.

"Annelie," Andy called but she waved him away again.

Andy had been tending bar long enough to handle problems on his own now.

Lukas needed to talk. She had seen it the moment he had sat down tonight, but the pub had been so busy that she hadn't been able to talk to him other than taking his order. He had never really spoken much about himself and the one time he needed to, she hadn't made time for him.

He had always made time to listen to her.

What sort of friend was she?

"I was wondering where you were." Her tone was jest but her heart meant the words, ached a little as the last three weeks caught up with her together with the revelation that she had been afraid of never seeing him again.

Lukas's eyes lifted back to meet hers, and she told herself not to read into the look that crossed his handsome face, because there was a chance she was misinterpreting it or just seeing what she wanted to see—that he was pleased to hear she had missed him, had been thinking about him.

He dropped his green gaze back to his whisky glass and ran a finger around the rim of it. "Sorry about that."

She never had been able to place his accent.

It wasn't British like hers and most of the people who frequented the pub.

She had asked him about it once and he had simply said that he had lived in many places. She had told him her whole life story and he hadn't even told her where he was from. If she asked again, would he tell her? If she didn't give up this time and tried to peel back his layers to learn more about him, would he answer all her questions?

She had never pressed him before, had secretly enjoyed the air of mystery that surrounded him, but now things were different. He had gone away, and had returned a different man, and she wanted to know where he had been, what he had done, and why he had disappeared. She wanted to know everything about him.

He picked up his glass and she took it from him.

"I think you've had enough of that." She tipped the contents in the sink behind the bar and stashed the glass there. "How are you getting home tonight?"

He frowned, propped his head up on his palm, and closed his eyes. "The usual way."

She shook her head at that. "I can't let you drive."

A smile curved his profane lips. "I don't drive. I fly."

"Well, I can't let you drink and fly." She couldn't contain the laugh that bubbled up, shook her head for a different reason as she looked at him.

He was drunk if he thought he could fly home.

Annelie covered his other hand with hers and he opened his eyes, their green depths meeting hers again. They were sharper now but not enough to satisfy her.

"I'll give you a lift if you wait until we've closed." Hopefully he would have sobered up a little by then and could direct her to his place.

She had never seen him outside work before and didn't have a clue about where he lived. She thought she remembered him mentioning it was in the city, somewhere close to the heart of London, but she couldn't be sure.

Lukas stared into her eyes for what felt like hours and then nodded.

Annelie took her hand back and smiled, relief flowing through her. It was better he didn't go home alone, in a cab or on the bus. She would only end up worrying that he had gotten into trouble somewhere.

Or might disappear again.

While she was driving him, she was going to get him to talk to her. She was going to find out where he had gone and why he was suddenly drinking. She was going to ease the weight on his shoulders just as he had done for her so many times in the past.

Closing time was only twenty minutes away, but it would be at least another hour before she had finished cleaning up, counting the takings and getting everything ready for tomorrow.

She glanced back at Lukas and debated making him a coffee to help him sober up.

He rested his arm on the counter and used it as a pillow, his eyes closing again. Sleep would probably help him as much as caffeine. He had looked tired before he had started drinking, worn down and in need of a good night's rest.

She turned towards the rows of bottles and optics and turned off the sound system, so only the chatter of the other patrons filled the pub. Hopefully the hum of voices wouldn't disturb Lukas.

Annelie flinched when Andy called for last orders, his voice loud enough to wake the neighbourhood, and scowled at him. He gave her a blank look. She jerked her chin towards Lukas where he was sleeping, and Andy's dark eyebrows lifted as his gaze shifted to him and then a mischievous smile lit his face as he looked back at her.

"He sleeping over?" Andy parked his hip against the bar near her as she served a customer.

"I'm taking him home." She shot Andy a look when he grinned at her. "It's not like that. I'm just going to drive him home and drop him off."

He didn't look as if he believed her.

"Just serve the customers." She shoved him playfully in his chest and he winked and went to work.

Her gaze crept back to Lukas, heart fluttering in her throat as she thought about driving him home and the way he had held her hand, had played with her fingers and had looked at her with a wicked edge to his eyes, a flare of desire that echoed inside her.

Did he want her, or was it just the booze talking?

She barely noticed the pub emptying, was too swept up in her thoughts to say goodbye to everyone as she got a head start on cleaning up.

"I'm out." Andy tossed his towel down at the other end of the bar. "You be good now."

Annelie ignored that. "Night."

He moved out from behind the bar, grabbed his coat and stopped behind Lukas.

She scowled at Andy when he clutched his hands together in front of his chest, twisted back and forth at the waist and fluttered his eyelashes as if he was swooning over Lukas.

"Get out of here before I fire your arse." She lifted her own towel, scrunched it up in her hand and threatened to throw it at him.

He grinned, turned on his heel and strode towards the door. "Don't do anything I wouldn't."

She shook her head. There wasn't much Andy wouldn't do.

The door closed and she shifted her focus to Lukas where he leaned over the bar, sound asleep. Her pulse thrummed, steadily picking up pace as she gazed at him and grew aware of the fact she was alone with him now.

Damn, he was gorgeous even when he was drunk, drew her to him like no other man had before him.

She shook herself out of her reverie, tied her long red hair back into a ponytail and wiped the bar down, doing her best not to disturb Lukas and trying to avoid looking at him.

It didn't work.

She found herself stood by him, looking down at his face, watching him sleep. A need poured through her, swirled and gained strength, until she couldn't resist it. She hesitated and then, with her heart in her mouth, brushed the tangled strands of his fair hair from his forehead.

His firm lips parted and he murmured something.

She smiled and brushed his skin again, lightly so he wouldn't wake, but enough contact to make her feel a little giddy.

When had she fallen for him?

It had come on so slowly over the past three years that she hadn't realised she had those sorts of feelings for Lukas until he had gone away, and then she had been worried that he wasn't coming back.

But here he was again, at her bar in the same stool he always occupied, bringing light into her life and her heart in that way only he could, making the days without him disappear.

A smile tugged at her lips. She had never been happier to see him.

Even if he was asleep.

He stirred and blinked slowly, as though trying to wake himself.

Annelie didn't take her hand back. She was feeling brave tonight, a little courageous and bold, willing to take a risk and see what happened.

"How are you feeling?" She combed her fingers through his hair.

Lukas frowned, his green eyes fixed on the distance, and then groaned. She took that as a negative answer.

"No better yet?" Her gaze followed her fingers as she stroked them down the curve of his left ear.

He nodded, moving her hand with him, and a smile touched his lips and then faded again when he closed his eyes.

"I'm almost done. I'll have you home soon." She went to walk away.

He caught her wrist so fast that it startled her, his grip firm as he sat up, and looked at her with such earnest eyes that her heart beat harder and a rush of nerves surged through her.

"I ever tell you that you're pretty?" Those words, spoken in a low husky voice, rocked her to her core.

Her pulse raced and her throat turned dry. She shook her head and he reached out with his other hand and ran the backs of his fingers down her cheek, his caress light but setting her nerve-endings aflame and sending a hot shiver over her skin. Her lips parted as she searched his eyes, trying to see if he knew what he was saying, and whether he believed she was pretty.

There was nothing but honesty and warmth in them.

They sparkled with it, looking brighter now even though the lights were lower, entrancing her. "Your beauty puts angels to shame."

Annelie tried to convince herself that it was the drink talking but failed dismally.

She had worked in the pub since she was in her early twenties, almost ten years ago, and had run it since her parents had retired early. She had enough experience to spot levels of inebriation.

Lukas's eyes were sharper and his words weren't slurred. He wasn't drunk anymore.

He was definitely still tipsy, but that excuse didn't hold with her heart. It believed him.

He really did think that she was beautiful.

She blushed. It burned her cheeks before she could get the better of herself. She worked at a bar. She was used to men telling her that she was beautiful at the end of the night, but the way Lukas said it, the fact that it was him, made her believe him.

"You really are." His hand slipped from her cheek to her jaw and he grazed his fingers along the curve of it. He smiled and her heart thudded. *He* was beautiful. She had never seen a man like him, with such deep green eyes and a smile that could make her heart pound and body tremble. "Beautiful."

"Hush." She took his hand away from her face and held it a moment. "Quit making me blush, Lukas."

His smile held. "I love the way you say my name. Say it again."

Annelie rolled her eyes. "Lukas."

"Not like that." He drew his hand towards him, luring her with it, until she was close to him. She stared down into his eyes, her mind racing forwards to contemplate things it shouldn't be. He wasn't going to kiss her. Even if he was looking more sober now, she couldn't let things go down that avenue. His eyes fell to her lips and then lifted to meet hers again. "Say it like you mean it. Like you said it just then."

Annelie looked deep into his eyes, lost in them and the way the flecks of pale gold seemed to shift and move against their emerald backdrop, and blinked slowly.

Her voice dropped to a whisper. "Lukas."

"Mmm, that's more like it." He pulled her closer and tilted his head.

Her gaze dropped to his mouth, heart hammering against her ribs and blood thundering as a need to kiss him bolted through her, lighting her up inside, making her sway towards him.

Just one kiss.

CHAPTER 2

Annelie broke free of Lukas instead of kissing him as she wanted, somehow managing to get control of herself.

Disappointment flashed across his face and she struggled to ignore it as she fiddled with her black t-shirt. He wasn't the only disappointed one. She had wanted to kiss him for so long now, had fantasised about the moment a thousand times over, but she couldn't.

No matter how tempting it was.

If she did, she would always wonder whether he had kissed her because he was half-drunk or whether he had kissed her because he felt something for her.

She wanted it to be because he felt something, the same way she felt about him, and that meant staying strong and resisting him.

She had foolishly kissed men before at the end of the night, falling foul of their flattery, the loneliness she felt at times driving her into their arms. She didn't want things to be like that with Lukas.

She wanted more than that.

"Let me finish cleaning and I'll take you home." She hurried away to the other end of the bar, not daring to look back at Lukas, not while she wanted to kiss him and was weak enough to go through with it.

By the time she had finished, Lukas was looking sober but tired.

And he was watching her.

Annelie could feel his eyes on her, following her around the room as she placed the chairs upside down on the tables. Heat seemed to follow wherever he looked, rippled over her skin and roused that need to kiss him, made her ache with a desire to go through with it. She wanted to throw caution to the wind, to take the risk and hope it would all work out.

She drifted over to Lukas, unable to resist the pull of him.

He turned on the stool to face her, his eyes holding the fire that burned within her, enticing her to kiss him after all.

She was feeling brave, wasn't she? Brave enough to reach out, grab him by his collar and kiss him?

She trembled at the thought, at the vision of him claiming her waist and pulling her against him as he seized command of the kiss.

He canted his head, his green eyes narrowing on her as the heat in them flared hotter.

It flared on her cheeks too, scalding them.

She cleared her throat, averted her gaze, and nodded towards the door.

"Come on." She didn't wait for him to get down off the stool.

She started towards the door and Lukas was soon beside her.

She snuck a glance at him and told herself it wasn't a crime to appreciate how damned good he always looked in the black shirt and jeans he wore. They hugged his figure just the right amount, giving subtle clues about how sexy the body they hid was and luring her into picturing him naked. Even when she shouldn't be.

She closed the door behind him and locked up.

"You okay?" She pocketed her keys and started down the quiet road with him towards the car park at the back of the pub, plucking the dead heads of a few flowers in the window boxes on the black painted sills of the elegant old white building as she passed.

It was nice to have company for once. The dark fronts of the shops that lined the road opposite the pub and eerie silence cut only by the sound of distant cars on the main road often sent a chill through her and made her race for the safety of her car.

With Lukas at her side, she didn't feel afraid.

She felt safe.

"I have been better." He tilted his head back, stared up at the night sky, and sighed, drawing her focus to him.

There was such a look of melancholy in his eyes. What was he thinking?

"Where did you go, Lukas?" Annelie took her car keys out of her pocket, turned the corner into the car park, and pressed the button on the fob. The lights on her small car flashed. "I really was worried about you."

Lukas stopped and looked at her.

She turned and met his gaze, letting him see that she wasn't just saying that. He had disappeared without a word and it had frightened her. She had missed him.

He stepped up to her, lifted his hand and gently cupped her cheek again, his palm warm against it, tearing down her defences and awakening the need to kiss him.

His eyes held hers and she swore she saw another flicker of affection in them.

Could he want her just as she wanted him?

"I had to go away. I should have told you, Annelie. I should not have worried you." There was black magic in his voice and the way he said her name, soft but with an underlying note of passion, and she was under his spell. He stroked her cheek, sending a shiver through her, and smiled into her eyes. "I did not think I would be gone so long. I promise I will not do it again."

Annelie told herself to break free but she couldn't.

She didn't want to.

She wanted to stand there in the warm night, feeling hot from head to toe because of Lukas's caress and the ardent look in his eyes. She wanted to believe that his words meant what she thought they did and that he liked her and things between them would be different now. She hadn't looked at another man since Lukas had walked into her life, had dreamed the impossible of him falling for her, and now it felt as though the impossible was possible after all.

Lukas wanted her as much as she wanted him.

She stepped into his embrace, her heart thundering against her chest, and stared up into his eyes.

His fingers stroked her neck, his thumb brushing over her chin and then under her jaw. He tilted her head back, his eyes fixed on hers, and lowered his mouth. She shivered when their lips met and then pressed her hands against his firm chest and melted into him as he kissed her. It started out slow, a bare meeting of lips, but before she could draw another breath, his mouth covered hers and he stole it away.

She tiptoed, slid her arms around his neck, and kissed him, shivered as their lips met and tongues traced each other in a sensual dance that stirred fire in her belly and her blood.

He groaned and it was music to her heart, driving her on.

She licked his lower lip, tangled her tongue with his, and kissed him harder, her breathing coming faster now as he held her closer. His palm cupped her nape, fingers pressing into her neck as he held her, kissed her deeper and harder still, igniting heat in her veins that quickly rolled to a boil.

Sense reared its ugly head but she shoved it away, not interested in anything her mind had to say on the matter. The kiss was divine. Lukas was divine. It didn't matter that he was still a little tipsy and that they were kissing in the middle of an unpleasant car park. She knew in her heart that this wasn't the drink talking.

He pulled back, breathing hard, and his eyes searched hers.

The fire in them matched the inferno burning within her.

Did she look so hungry too?

She wanted to devour him.

"Annelie..." he started and looked as though he was going to kiss her again, but then he stepped back. "I am sorry. If I have offended—"

"No."

His eyes darted to hers.

She fought to voice what was in her heart. She wanted him too. She had wanted that kiss more than anything. She was on the brink of saying it but other words came out instead.

"We should get you home."

Disappointment flickered across his face again and his gaze went back to the sky as he gave a subtle nod.

Annelie walked to her car, cursing herself as cold swept through her, the same disappointment that had shone in his eyes. She ached all over to feel his hands and lips on her again, longed for him to hold her close and never let her go.

What was wrong with her?

Why couldn't she have just said what she had wanted to?

Lukas, it was fine that you kissed me because I want to do that to you and a lot more besides.

It was so easy to say it in her head.

She walked around the car and glanced at him. His eyes were on her again, drifting over her body, bringing the fire back in their wake. She burned for him. She burned so much that she felt as though she was going to die if he didn't touch her and kiss her again, if he didn't quench the flames as only he could.

If she had said what she had wanted to, would he be kissing her again now? Would that divine body be against hers and his hands be on her, skimming over her in the way she was craving, bringing her to life with passion and need?

Just thinking about that was too much to bear, had her aching again, on the verge of doing something crazy.

Annelie yanked the car door open instead and got in, gripped the steering wheel to anchor herself in place and stop her from grabbing hold of Lukas as he slid into the passenger seat beside her. She mentally cursed herself for letting her nerve fail her.

She started the engine, put the car into gear and drove, needing something to distract her from her turbulent thoughts and the need blazing inside her.

She needed a distraction, but Lukas didn't offer one.

He was quiet, only speaking to give her directions across London to where he lived. When they reached it, she pulled the car to a halt in a space outside and stared at the building.

A beautiful pale four-storey Georgian townhouse.

"You live *here*?" She couldn't quite bring herself to believe it.

She had never figured Lukas for a moneyed type. He had never once looked as though he had more than a few hundred pounds to his name.

Lukas nodded and got out of the car, not waiting for her.

Had she put him in a bad mood?

She had definitely put herself in a bad mood by resisting him. She cursed herself again. She should have just kissed him. She should have kissed him so hard he would have had no doubt that she wanted him, that his kiss hadn't offended her or anything like that. It had caught her off guard, had been so damned good that she hadn't been able to think straight at the time, but now her head was clear and she wanted to kiss him again.

Her eyes tracked him. He was walking in a straight line, not wavering at all, and seemed sober now. If he kissed her again, she wouldn't be able to resist him. She wouldn't have a reason to.

Annelie stepped out, locked her car, and hurried across the quiet road to him. He waited on the golden-lit porch of the building, in front of the black door, his gaze drilling into her again, stoking the embers of the fire he had ignited in her.

She stopped at the bottom of the steps, waiting for him to say something.

All he had to do was invite her in. If he invited her in, she would take it as a sign that she hadn't messed anything up and that he still wanted her.

His eyes held hers for what felt like hours and then he spoke in a low, hushed voice that did strange things to her insides, made her feel light and a little hazy.

"I just want to be clear about one thing. I did not kiss you because of the drink." He glanced away and then met her gaze again, his green eyes sharp and focused on her, so intense they sent a thrill through her. "There is a reason I like to sit at the bar and talk to you, Annelie. There is a reason I kissed you."

He looked as though he wanted to say more but she didn't give him a chance.

She ran up the steps, threw her arms around his neck and kissed him again.

He stumbled backwards into the door, wrapped his arms around her waist and lifted her up his body as his tongue stroked the seam of her lips. She opened for him, shivered as their tongues touched and she fought him for dominance. An ache started low in her belly, the heat gathering there as she kissed him, savoured the taste of him and the warmth of his hard body against hers.

It was Heaven. A moan slipped from her lips.

Lukas fumbled with the door behind him and they fell into the bright entrance hall. She giggled as he stumbled and held her closer, kept kissing the breath from her as if he couldn't get enough. She definitely couldn't get enough of him.

She moaned and kissed him deeper, itching with a need for more, to satisfy this hunger he stirred in her. She poured her passion and need into it, until it wrenched control from her and the kiss turned choppy and rough, a fierce meeting of lips that tore a groan from Lukas.

A wave of scorching heat swept through her at the sound of it.

She gasped into his mouth when he grabbed her backside with both hands, his grip on it firm, fingers digging into her buttocks through her jeans. She hopped up and wrapped her legs around his waist and he hit the wall with her, pinning her there with his body.

She trembled as images of them tangled together, naked and wild, flashed through her mind. She wanted all of them to happen right now, this instant, wanted to live out every hot dream she had ever had about Lukas.

"Which floor?" She managed between kisses, too hungry for him to break contact for more than a second.

"Third." There was a laugh to his voice that brought out her smile.

He kissed her again and turned with her, heading for the stairs. Was he serious? He couldn't carry her all the way to the third floor while kissing her.

Lukas seemed intent on proving her wrong. He held on to her, his hands grasping her backside, his body shifting between her hips in the most delicious way, and kissed along her jaw as he took the steps two at a time.

Annelie didn't pay the slightest bit of attention to her surroundings.

All she could think about was what would happen when they reached his apartment and how good it felt to be in his arms. She kissed his throat, earning quiet moans from him whenever she nipped it with her teeth or sucked. The rougher she was, the louder he groaned, and it drove her on, making her want to bite him harder.

She wriggled against him, hot all over, and moaned when he nibbled her neck, kissing and licking it, getting his revenge by sending shivers dancing over her skin and stoking the fire of her hunger for him. She leaned her head back and he held her closer, devouring her throat, taking her higher and higher, and not only towards his apartment.

"Almost there," he whispered into her mouth and her temperature soared with anticipation.

He kissed her throat, her cheeks, and then her lips, paused against her mouth and said the one thing guaranteed to shatter her restraint, the one thing she had wanted to hear above all else.

He breathed it against her lips in a husky voice, turning three simple words into the most erotic thing she had ever heard.

"I want you."

Annelie stilled in his strong arms, the force of her need and his passion colliding to leave her trembling as she waged war with herself, fighting to regain control that she knew she would never be able to claw back now.

She let go instead, let all the desire she had bottled up over the past few years rush to the fore and consume her.

Because she wanted him too.

And she was damn well going to have him.

CHAPTER 3

Annelie squeaked as she hit the deep blue covers of the double bed in the middle of the large and elegant low-lit bedroom. She bounced on the mattress, her eyes on the high ceiling, and moaned when Lukas covered her, his body pressing delightfully into hers. She wrapped her arms back around his neck and kissed him again, her eyes closing and her heart crying out for more as he pinned her beneath him.

His tongue delved between her lips and she opened for him, moaned as he kissed her deeper and burrowed his hand into her flame-red hair to hold her against him. She stilled beneath him, surrendering to him and savouring the heat of his kiss and the way each brush of their lips had flames skittering over her skin beneath her clothing.

He groaned, pressed his knee between her thighs and then followed it with his other one. He clutched her tighter and shifted his hips against hers, tearing another moan from her throat as his hard cock rubbed her through her jeans.

She wished they were naked, flesh-to-flesh.

Lukas moaned into her mouth, kissed her fiercely, savagely, and then broke away from her lips. She clutched his shoulders, twisting his black shirt into her fists, a need to stop him and force him to kiss her again pounding through her.

That need washed away when he swept his lips down her jaw to her neck, buried his face there and devoured her sensitive flesh with hungry open-mouthed kisses. She dug her fingers through his sandy hair, clinging to him, and lifted her knee so it grazed his hip, unable to keep still as he sent wave after wave of shivers dancing over her body.

She wanted more.

She wanted all of him.

Needed it.

A sigh escaped her as he lowered his hands, caught the hem of her black baby-doll tee and shoved it up over her breasts. His actions were rough, frantic, as he pulled the t-shirt off over her head and she matched him as she gained some space, grabbing his black shirt and pulling on it before he could kiss her or touch her again.

He sat back on his heels between her legs and pulled his shirt off, tossing it aside as his gaze burned into her, the heat and hunger in it setting her aflame.

Annelie paused.

Her breath hitched in her throat.

In front of her knelt a god.

She ran her gaze over his taut torso, absorbing every nuance of his muscles as they shifted with his breathing, on the verge of purring over the sight of him alone. She could feel his eyes on her, running over her chest and her stomach, taking her in as she took him in.

They were both still a moment, lost in a trance that felt too powerful to break free from, and then Lukas was on her again, shattering the hold the delicious sight of him had had on her.

His bare chest pressed against hers, the skin-on-skin contact thrilling her as his lips captured hers and she lost herself in the kiss and the feel of him. She ran her fingers over his side, across his back, unable to resist the need to explore the strong muscles and warm skin that was hers to play with now.

She had ached for this for so long.

She charted every inch of him that she could reach as she kissed him, her tongue caressing his, trying to slow the pace of his passion even when it felt impossible, as though she was trying to tell the tides to stop surging.

He broke away from her lips, gripped her hip in his left hand and thrust against her as he kissed her cheek and jaw, and nipped at her throat.

She groaned at the too-light contact between them, her jeans and his making it less than it should have been.

Less than she desperately needed.

It seemed he didn't approve either because he was suddenly kissing down over her chest.

She arched upwards as he slid his hands beneath her and her eyes fluttered shut again as he unhooked her black bra and removed it. Cool air caressed her breasts, blissful against her overheating flesh. She moaned, writhed as she grew restless with a need to feel Lukas's hands on her again. His mouth on her.

He covered her left breast with his hand, thumbing her nipple and sending sparks shooting outwards from it, and groaned as he lowered his head and tugged her other nipple into his mouth.

She jerked upwards, pressing her breasts against his hand and his mouth as bliss shot through her, cranking her tighter.

He groaned again and swirled his tongue around her nipple before sucking it, torturing her with the feel of his mouth on her. She sighed, arched her back, and held his head against her breasts. This was what she had been dying to feel.

"Lukas." His name left her lips before she could stop it and her cheeks blazed over the heated way it had come out.

He moaned and held her closer, sliding his hand from her breast and down her side to her bottom. He grasped her hip and thrust, rubbing his caged erection against her most sensitive spot and driving her wild.

She needed him naked.

Now.

Her hands drifted over his back as she fought the temptation to push him off her so she could get him naked, forcing herself to remain where she was and surrender to him instead, to trust that whatever he had planned, it would scratch every itch she had.

The rushed pace of her hands slowed when he moved, his muscles shifting beneath his soft skin. He felt so good. She could spend hours just stroking him but it would have to come later. Right now, the fierce need inside her was only getting worse and she couldn't wait anymore. There were parts of him she hadn't explored yet, one in particular she often admired whenever he came to the pub.

She skimmed her hands over the small of his back, and the twin dimples there, and stretched to reach his bottom so she could see if it felt as good as it looked.

Lukas foiled her plans.

He moved downwards, kissing over her stomach, distracting her from whining when he moved out of reach. She sighed again when his hands settled on the belt of her jeans and let her arms fall to her sides, surrendering to him once again, letting him have his way with her.

He made fast work of her belt, removed her trainers, and then tugged her jeans down and off.

She heard him move and opened her eyes, a need to see what he was doing racing through her.

His green gaze met hers and he smiled as he fingered his own belt.

Her hungry eyes fell to his hands, her breath seizing in her throat and heat flashing through her as he slowly popped the buttons of his jeans and opened his fly, eased them down his hips and revealed himself to her.

She wriggled, impatient and restless as her eyes stopped on his hard cock as it jutted from his nest of pale curls.

She wanted that. Now.

Lukas kicked off his jeans and she reached a hand out to him, smiling shyly, wanting him to come to her.

In her.

She wanted to feel him inside her, to live out her dreams with the object of them.

He pressed one knee into the mattress, leaned over her and took hold of her hips. She gasped when he pushed her up the bed until her head hit the pillows, his body corded perfection as his muscles flexed. His gaze fell to her thighs and he frowned, looking like a man starved, and then hooked his fingers into the hem of her knickers and pulled them off.

Annelie didn't want to close her eyes, she wanted to keep them open and see this was more than a dream, but she couldn't stop them from slipping shut as Lukas parted her thighs and feathered a lone finger up the length of her plush mound.

She moaned, writhed, and sighed, aching for more, unsure whether she could handle it but needing it all the same.

He didn't disappoint.

He touched her again, caressing her with two fingers now, teasing her pert bead and slick core, forcing the anticipation within her to rise beyond her control. She tilted her head back into the pillows and clutched the blue bedcovers, bunching them into her fists.

"Lukas."

"I do love the way you say my name," he husked, voice scraping low and sexy, devastating her.

A blush blazed through her from her toes right up to her head, but she didn't care. She couldn't stop herself from moaning his name whenever he stroked her, teasing her and making hunger coil in her stomach. Her whole body felt tight and she was close to pleading him by the time she felt the bed depress.

She gasped at the first flick of his tongue over her swollen arousal and clutched the bedclothes tighter, desperate not to climax instantly. She was too hungry for him, the years of fantasising about him and this moment wrecking her ability to control herself.

He moaned and she followed suit, the sound of his pleasure bringing out her own. She let go of her inhibitions and embraced her passion when he flicked her bead with his tongue again and then suckled.

"Lukas." Annelie screwed her eyes shut, twisted the covers in her fists and resisted the temptation to seize hold of his head, to twine her fingers in his tousled blond locks and hold him against her.

Each sweep of his tongue sent sparks skittering along her nerves, racing outwards from her hips, stoking the fire inside her. She could barely stop herself from bucking her hips against his face and riding his tongue. She wanted more. Needed more.

"Say it again." He swirled his tongue around her and she could only oblige.

"Lukas!"

He groaned and her eyes shot open when he slid a finger into her warm core, thrusting it deep. She was in Heaven. Sweet damn Heaven as he pumped her with it, slow and steady, maddening her with the teasing pace and the sweep of his tongue over her nub. What little control she had managed to retain shattered and she couldn't stop herself from thrusting with him, riding his finger as her breaths came faster, the tension inside her building to a staggering high. He moaned again when her muscles clenched him and then slid a second finger into her, stretching her.

She wanted his cock in her. She wanted to feel that stretching her. Just the memory of how hard and good it had looked when she had caught a glimpse of it had her ready to come undone.

Her hands found her breasts and she teased her nipples, pushing herself towards a release that she desperately wanted. She rode Lukas's fingers as he plunged deeper, harder, his mouth teasing her as he rubbed her in just the right spot.

And then went completely still.

Annelie groaned her disapproval.

It became a growl of frustration when he pulled his fingers out of her.

She opened her eyes, ready to berate him and make him touch her again, because she needed release now, was too far gone.

She stilled, her angry words dying on her lips as Lukas prowled up the length of her. She glanced down at his hard length, needing to see it again. A low moan fell from her lips as Lukas stroked his right hand down the shaft, exposing the blunt crown. It was wet, glistened with his arousal, and another moan slipped from her as her body pulsed in response to the sight of it.

She wanted that. She was going to have it.

He settled his hips against hers, thrusting the length of his cock against her, rubbing her sensitive bead with it and threatening to push her over the edge. She didn't want that now. She wanted to find release when he was inside her.

She looped her arms around his neck and looked up into his eyes, and the burning need she felt drifted into the background as she fell into them and he stilled above her.

He had the strangest expression on his gorgeous face and she again had the impression that he wanted to say something, and then he kissed her and chased her thoughts away.

"Annelie," he whispered against her lips, the sound of it teasing her as much as his hard length. She moaned her response, too lost in the feel of him against her, kissing her, to say anything. "I want you."

The force of those words stole her breath again.

If he wanted her, he could have her. She wasn't going anywhere. She was gasping to have him inside her, for him to quell the raging inferno that he had ignited within her and had let burn without end these past three years. She raised her hips to his, encouraging him to do it.

He shifted his hips back and the tip of his cock nudged against her. She groaned as he eased it down, stroking her flesh, and raised her hips. He pressed forwards and another moan escaped her as he fed every delicious inch of him into her, stretching her body. Her eyes drifted shut as she savoured the feel of it and then opened again when he was as deep as she could take him.

Lukas remained there a moment, their bodies intimately locked and his face level with hers. He brushed the hair from her face, his fingers lightly stroking her brow and her cheek, and his eyes fixed on hers.

Annelie mirrored his actions, sweeping the messy strands of his fair hair from his forehead, enjoying the quiet moment of intimacy.

Now that he was inside her, she felt calm and oddly at peace.

Looking into his eyes made her feel that way sometimes, especially when she was picking out every golden fleck as she was now.

"Lukas." She ran her finger across his lower lip and he smiled.

"Annelie." He dipped his head and claimed her mouth.

The fire returned when he eased his hips back, slowly drawing his cock out of her, and thrust back in. She wrapped her arms around his neck, twisted his hair around her fingers, and kissed him as he pumped her with his hard length, moving deep with long strokes that tore breathy moans from her. He hooked his hands over her shoulders and plunged harder into her body as he curled his hips, stoking the fire until it threatened to consume her. She uttered his name into his mouth, clutching him, her whole body tightening from the feel of him thrusting into her, fusing their bodies as one and stealing her breath away.

He broke away from her mouth and kissed her neck and she trembled as he groaned. His hot breath washed over her throat between kisses, her name falling from his lips in time with each plunge of his body into hers.

He grunted and thrust faster, his hips pumping hard, the pace quickening until it became frantic again. Annelie raised her hips, holding Lukas to her throat, loving the way he groaned into it and covered it with hot passionate kisses. His fingers dug into her shoulders and she ran her hands down his back, to his bottom, encouraging him to go faster and take her. She wanted it rougher, quicker, a violent coupling that matched the need and desire burning through her veins like molten lava.

Lukas lowered one hand to her hips, lifted them off the bed, and gave her what she needed.

He filled her hard and fast, deep jerking movements that had sparks shooting over her abdomen with each meeting of their hips. She screwed her eyes shut and moaned, clutching his backside, reaching for her climax. Her belly tightened, her body clenching his each time he filled her, and she could almost reach it.

Her heart thundered, blood rushing through her, and she tilted her head back, her mouth wide open. Lukas moaned into her ear, his breathing as hard and rough as his thrusts.

"More." She screwed her face up. "More."

She tensed her muscles around his hard length and her eyes shot open when he thrust deep into her and a wave of pleasure exploded through her. She gasped as hot sparks swept over her quivering thighs, her entire body quaking as release rushed through every inch of her.

Lukas groaned deeper. She dug her fingertips into his backside, urging him towards his own release, moaning as he drew out her climax with every delicious plunge of his cock into her. He grunted with each hard thrust, his grip on her growing painful as he held her hip and her shoulder, and his hips jerking frantically.

Her name fell from his lips, uttered in a low voice as he drove deep into her warm trembling core and froze, his entire body tensed as his cock pulsed, shooting hot jets of his seed into her. He stayed there a moment, rigid and motionless, and then moaned and shifted, pressing a little deeper still as he collapsed on top of her.

Annelie wrapped her arms around him, her fast breathing matching his, and tried to gather herself. He was heavy against her but she didn't mind. His cock continued to pulse and twitch, and she liked the feel of it, the feel of him inside her, completing her.

She slowly opened her eyes and stroked his back as she pieced herself back together and absorbed the feel of him, and what they had just done.

She frowned when the world came back into focus and she noticed a dark pink line on his shoulder. At first, she thought that she had scratched him, but when she looked closer, she realised that it was a scar, and it was recent. She stroked the line of it where it started on his back and ran over the curve of his shoulder.

He murmured something against her neck and sighed. His racing heart pounded against her chest, gradually slowing as she caressed him.

Annelie craned her neck and looked down his back.

Her frown returned.

There were other scars on it—all of them long deep pink lines.

She stroked a few of them and then her wandering fingers found ones that made her pause. There were two thick scars, both at least the length of her forearm, one on each shoulder blade, following the line of his spine.

What had happened to him?

She nudged Lukas, wanting to ask, and he groaned. The weight of him against her and his slow breathing told her that she wasn't going to get an answer tonight. He had fallen asleep.

Annelie rolled him off her.

He frowned in his sleep and sprawled out on the bed, stark naked, as though he didn't have a care in the world and didn't mind if people saw him nude.

She wished she could be like that. She looked around the low-lit blue bedroom and spotted a white panelled door. It had to be the bathroom. She slipped from the bed, hurried over to it, and opened it. A white tiled bathroom was on the other side. She turned on the light and closed the door. Her reflection looked pale from the bright light but her cheeks were still crimson.

She grabbed some tissues and cleaned herself up. Perhaps she should have asked him whether he had a condom. She didn't really know that much about him and it wasn't like her to have unprotected sex, even when she was on the pill. But it was Lukas. How many times had he been in her dreams, in her fantasies? Now they were all reality.

A smile curved her lips and she finished up and went back into the bedroom. Lukas lay on his side now, snoring quietly. He had said that it was more than alcohol, that she was beautiful and he wanted her. She believed him. She just wasn't sure where this was going to lead.

What if he changed his mind in the morning and was a different person?

She pushed her fears away, crept onto the bed behind him, and stroked the scars on his back.

In the morning, she would ask him what was going to happen now.

Her fingers caressed the darkest thickest scars over his shoulder blades.

And she would ask him what had happened to him.

CHAPTER 4

It was morning.

Lukas could feel the sun outside, calling him with false promises of vaulted blue heavens in which he could fly. He couldn't do that anymore. They had even taken that from him. His chest tightened at the thought of never flying again but he buried his pain deep, refusing to let it master him and tear all hope from him.

It wasn't difficult when his head was pounding and sore.

Something touched his back, stroking it lightly and with care.

There was love in that caress, and concern, a sensation that was foreign and new to him, and bewitching.

He tried to gather his scattered thoughts and senses so he could focus on the person behind him.

Impossible.

Her fingers felt good against him, soothing his raging head and bringing back memories of last night and being with her. Bliss. Being with her had been nothing short of bliss. He wanted to experience it all again, ached with that need as he let her explore him and savoured the tenderness of her touch as her fingers drifted over his right deltoid and then skimmed the top of his shoulder. Heat followed in their wake, a fire that sizzled and scalded him, had him burning with a fierce desire to roll to face her and kiss her again, to lose himself in her and forget everything else existed.

She feathered her fingertips down the line of his spine and up to his right shoulder blade.

An itch ignited there, mounted so swiftly that he stiffened and panicked.

No.

Lukas tried to focus but it was too late.

The urge drove through him, brought out by her teasing fingers and tender touch, and he couldn't contain it. He gritted his teeth, fought with all his might, but she swept her hand across his shoulder blade again and it was game over.

"Don't." He started to move away, unsure whether he was talking to her or his wings, but he wasn't quick enough.

His wings erupted from his back so fast that it hurt, struck her hard and knocked her off the bed.

She hit the floor with a thud.

No.

Lukas scrambled to his knees and twisted to face her. His white wings caught the lamp on the bedside table and he grimaced as it toppled off and smashed.

Annelie sat nude on the wooden floor, her hands splayed behind her, her chocolate eyes wide and her face ashen as she stared up at him.

He loosed a low growl of frustration and reached for her.

Her gaze leaped from his wings to his face, and he saw in her eyes the moment shock turned to fear, to panic that had her launching to her feet. She shook her head as she bolted for the bedroom door, her fear flooding the room and him.

Lukas kicked off, scrambling across the bed to reach the door before her, because he couldn't let her run. He needed to explain, to ease her fear and put her mind at rest. He couldn't let her leave.

He needed her too much.

His bare feet hit the floor and the cold prickle of fear that she would leave him faded as he reached the door first. He frowned as his head spun, skull aching as if a demon gripped it and was attempting to squeeze his brain out of it, and turned to face her just as she reached him. He blocked the way, jamming his hands against the doorframe and using his wings as a barricade. It didn't deter her. She tried to pass him and when he moved to counter her, keeping her contained, she bit out a curse and shoved at his bare chest.

He grabbed her wrists.

"Let me go." She snatched her hands back and tried to pass him again, diving to her right and dipping low.

She ducked under his arm as he reached for her and almost made it past him.

He twisted, caught her around the waist from behind and pulled her against him as she struggled. His body got the wrong idea when her soft warm backside brushed his groin. Getting an erection was not going to help matters.

He turned with her so she was back in the bedroom.

She scratched his arm, elbowed him in the ribs so hard his breath actually left him, and ran towards the bed when he released her, because manhandling her was getting him nowhere and he didn't want her to be afraid of him. He didn't want to hurt her. He just wanted her to listen to him, to give him a chance to explain.

"Annelie." Lukas furled his white wings against his back and gentled his tone, hoping to soothe her.

She ignored him, grabbing her clothes and throwing them on. Her black t-shirt was backwards but he didn't think she would appreciate him mentioning it when she was panicking. She clawed her long red hair back into a rough ponytail, eyed him warily and then dashed forwards, making another attempt to duck under his arm.

He grabbed her again, because as much as he didn't want to scare her or hurt her, he couldn't let her walk out of the door. If she did that now, he would never see her again.

"I can explain." Lukas wasn't quite sure what he intended to tell her but it sounded like the right thing to say in a situation that was rapidly going downhill.

"Explain what... that I'm going crazy or that I just slept with an angel?" Annelie gave up trying to get past him and backed away. "I think I've gone insane... or at least I hope I have."

When the backs of her legs hit the end of the mattress, she sank onto it and stared at him.

He focused on her, trying to detect her feelings. They were all over the place. Angels had acute senses but he couldn't tell whether she was angry or petrified. Maybe it was a little of both.

She leaned forwards, rested her elbows on her knees, and buried her face in her hands. "I'm going to Hell."

"No, you won't... Annelie... look at me." He wanted to reach for her, ached with a need to touch her and calm her, to feel her and know he hadn't messed everything up. Somehow, he found the strength to hold himself back, to give her the space she clearly needed.

"I'd rather not." She grabbed the blue duvet and pulled it over her head.

Lukas sighed and scrubbed a hand down over his face as he racked his brain. What could he say that wouldn't inflame things? There had to be something he could say to her that would go some way towards repairing the damage the sudden appearance of his wings had done.

"I'm sorry." It was the only thing that came to him, and it fell from his lips filled with sincerity, honesty and resignation he hoped she would hear through the bedclothes she was hiding under.

She emerged from the blanket and shook her head, the disbelief still written across her face.

When she looked down at her arm and pinched it, he frowned at her.

"What are you doing?" His gaze darted between her face and her arm as she pinched it again.

"Trying to wake up. This has to be a dream." She gave her arm another pinch and dismay crossed her face when she looked at him. She paled. "God, this is real... the wings are real... you're an angel... and I just blasphemed... and I *slept* with you!"

His shoulders sagged as her feelings came through loud and clear despite the riot in his head.

She was angry with him.

He could understand that, even when he didn't want to, wanted to pretend she had no reason to be angry with him. He couldn't change what had happened though, and as wicked as it was of him, even if he could, if he could turn back time to last night and do things over, he still wouldn't tell her. He wouldn't trade what had been a night right out of his dreams for her fleeing from him when he announced he needed to tell her something before things went too far and confessed he was an angel.

It was difficult to concentrate as his head pounded but he managed it somehow and his wings slowly shrank and disappeared into his back.

Annelie looked as horrified on seeing them disappear as she had on seeing them appear. Her heart raced in his mind and no matter what angle he looked at it from, the situation showed no sign of improving.

"It is not a dream, and it is not a sin." It was the bane of all his kind that mortals thought they were off limits, saints who couldn't enjoy life in the way a human could.

That belief couldn't be further from the truth.

They had rules, laws they had to obey, but all angels were fun and frivolous creatures when they weren't on duty, and many of them had fallen in love with mortals.

Just as he was in love with her.

He hadn't realised it until he had gone away.

Before then, he had merely thought that she was pretty, easy to talk to, interesting and someone who eased his loneliness. A friend.

Going away had made him realise that he had been falling for her since first setting eyes on her.

If he told her that now, would it fix anything? Would she still hate him? Would it make everything worse?

He wasn't sure that was possible.

"Annelie?"

She didn't seem to be listening. She was staring at his shoulders, as though waiting for his wings to appear again, her dark eyes large and mouth hanging open. It was a struggle to keep them away but he had to do it, no matter how much they wanted to come out again and how much his head hurt.

Drinking had been a bad idea.

But then, it had been the only way of erasing his pain, and humans always seemed to use drink to cope with things. The position he was in right now, another black mark against him probably wouldn't mean much. It would only damage his pride.

Whatever pride he had left anyway.

He laughed bitterly. "I am not even an angel at the moment... I haven't been since the night we met."

Her dark eyes met his and confusion shone in them as her fine eyebrows furrowed.

It hurt him to think about the past three years.

He wasn't sure he would have made it through them without Annelie.

She had been the one good thing in his world, the light in his darkest times, had given him friendship and support that had eased his suffering and had made his pain bearable. She had given him hope. She had given him courage. Without ever knowing what he was, or what he had been through, she had done everything right, had buoyed him and stopped him from sinking into the mire of his pain.

He felt sure that without her in his life, he would have sunk into despair and would have been tempted to the other side, into the darkness of Hell to serve a new master.

He feared that might happen now, because he felt sure she was going to leave and he would never see her again, and he needed her more than ever.

Things had never been this bad for him.

She couldn't leave. She was the only good thing left in his world. She was the only one keeping him from slipping and completing his fall from grace.

"Funny... you have wings like an angel." Annelie stood and stepped closer to him.

Her heart still raced, rushing in his head, speaking of her fear, but it didn't stop her from braving another tentative step forwards. She cast her gaze over him, from head to toe and back again.

"Wings I cannot use." Those words falling from his lips made it hit home that his ability to fly had been stripped from him. Worse, they had let him keep his wings, tempting him to use them. If he did, he would be punished.

His chest burned with the pain of being denied the one thing that had given him comfort and a sliver of hope, had made him believe things were going to turn out fine if he only held on for long enough.

Because they hadn't taken his wings from him.

Only now they had.

And as it hit him hard all over again, his strength drained from him, flowed out of him so quickly his legs felt as if they would give out beneath him.

He leaned against the doorframe, sinking into it for support as his stomach turned and heart ached.

What hope was there for him now?

He knew what happened next. He had seen angels judged, had witnessed them stripped of their wings, and none of them had chosen a mortal life. Anger and pain had consumed them, the effect of having their home and their purpose taken from them swift to destroy them and send them into the waiting arms of the Devil.

Would he complete his fall?

He looked down at his bare feet, at the wooden floorboards, seeing beyond them to the dark realm that existed below him, hidden by layers of rock from mortal eyes. It was there though, he could feel it already heating the soles of his feet, could feel the tug towards the darkness.

"I am... fallen... I think you mortals call it." Lukas closed his eyes, clenched his jaw and steeled himself, refusing to succumb to the temptation of exchanging his white wings for crimson ones in service of the Devil and fighting to deny the pain that whirled inside him like a storm, gathering speed to tear at him and threaten to pull him apart completely. It rushed through him, filled him with despair and sorrow, and anger too. "I was banished here three years ago... and three weeks ago I went to appeal against my sentence and make them see the truth."

"The truth?" Her voice was quiet, cautious, but the sound of it spread warmth through his veins that helped him fight the pain and the temptation of the Devil.

He opened his eyes and looked at her, resting his head against the wooden frame.

"I did not commit the crime that I am being punished for." He searched her eyes, wishing that she would show a sign of compassion, or affection, something other than anger and hurt. He needed to see something warm in her, something to give him a thread of hope to hold on to. "I wanted to tell you so many times."

"That you were falsely accused?" Her eyebrows pinched and she canted her head, and he wanted to find relief in the fact that she looked calmer now, felt more at ease around him, but he didn't dare do it, was afraid that if he did, she would only hurt him more when she walked out of the door.

He smiled at her confusion but it lasted only a second before sorrow and hurt welled up to steal it from his lips. "That I am an angel."

"Why?" Her dark gaze darted between his eyes and her heart began to settle at last, her fear beginning to fade.

That need to reach out and touch her, to caress her cheek and know that he hadn't messed everything up between them, consumed him again, but it was another thing he didn't dare go through with. It would only scare her away. He had to take things slowly, needed to rebuild the trust between them by opening himself to her and letting her see that he was being honest with her, and that he was sorry for how things had gone.

"Because... I hate lying to you. I hate hiding things from you." Lukas pinched the bridge of his nose and closed his eyes again. He drew down a long breath, held it for a moment and then exhaled it on a sigh, trying to push his pain out with it so he could focus on the moment and making things right with Annelie. If that was possible. It had to be. "Because I want you to know me."

"Why?"

Was that the only question she had for him?

He deserved her anger, and her disbelief, and he was prepared for it. He had always known it would be impossible to tell her that he was an angel without going through this. Even if he had found a way to break it to her gently, she still would have thought she was going insane and would have struggled to believe what she was seeing.

Lukas opened his eyes and stared at her feet. She had moved closer. Her small bare feet made him smile despite the pain beating in his heart. They were so delicate. Everything about her was delicate and soft. He loved her for that. He loved her for her smile and how open she was with him, and how she always found time to speak to him.

"I meant what I said last night, Annelie." His gaze met hers again and he stepped away from the door, towards her, closing the gap between them.

His head ached but the pain in his heart eclipsed it.

He didn't want her to leave, and if baring his soul was the only way of making her stay, then he was willing to go through that. He was willing to risk her breaking his heart. It would be the last straw for him, and he would no longer have a reason not to fall into darkness and live up to the name of a fallen angel, but it was a chance that he had to take.

"There is a reason that I come to the pub and sit on that stool and talk to you... and I think you know what that reason is." He searched her eyes, needing to see in them that she did know the reason he came to see her as often as he could.

Those alluring rich chocolate eyes widened, her cheeks coloured and she dropped her gaze.

Lukas hesitated a moment, struggled to resist the need that poured through him and failed. He couldn't stop himself from gently placing his fingers under her jaw, even when his head and heart screamed that he would scare her away, that he was moving too fast again.

His fingers shook so much that he was sure that she would notice.

So much rested on this touch. If she accepted it, he would take it as a sign that there was hope for him, and for them. If she pushed him away, he wasn't sure what he would do.

She remained still, her gaze downcast, but she didn't shirk his touch.

Lukas sucked down a deep trembling breath and raised her head. Her eyes slowly lifted, skimming up his neck and then over his lips, coming to meet his. The look in them said that she knew all too well what he was talking about and that he hadn't misjudged her feelings.

He wasn't the only one who had fallen in love over the past three years.

She had never once spoken to him about men, had never been out on dates, had always smiled at him in a way she never did with other men, always laughed and found a way to touch his hands.

She was in love with him too.

But there was a barrier between them, one that he couldn't push her to break through.

It was her decision. It had to be.

He wasn't mortal and she had to accept that. She had to come to understand his kind and his world, and see whether she could still love him or whether she had to move on. All he could do was try to convince her that it would be worth it if she stayed with him, and that he wanted her more than anything.

More than flying?

He wasn't sure of that yet. He had a decision to make too, one that depended on hers.

His wings pushed to break free again but he held them at bay, wrestling for control. It was difficult enough under normal circumstances to hide them. The headache from the drink was making it almost impossible. He couldn't let them out though. Annelie was slowly growing closer to him again and he was sure it was because she couldn't see his wings. She only saw a man before her, and he needed to keep it that way until she was comfortable around him again.

If she saw his wings, she would probably go back to wanting to run from him.

Lukas took his hand back and rubbed his eyes.

"I guess now I know why you're such a good listener." Her sweet voice wrapped around him, soothing the ache in his skull.

He shook his head. "I am only a good listener for you. I am a lousy listener for others. It wasn't my specialty."

"Angels have specialties?" A frown pinched her eyebrows again and then she quickly shook her head and held her hands up in front of her. "Actually, I don't think I want to know. I still feel as though I'm dreaming all of this."

That wasn't good. He had been hoping she had been coming to terms with things, with him.

"What can I do to make you see that this is real, Annelie, and that I mean you no harm?" He wanted to reach for her again, to take hold of her hands and keep her with him, but resisted the need, because pushing her would get him nowhere.

A smile touched her lips, shy and sweet. "I don't think you'll hurt me."

"I already did." Lukas's heart beat harder when she met his gaze and held it.

There was a hint of warmth in her dark eyes and no fear. She wasn't lying. She really did believe that he wouldn't harm her.

"I was just shocked." She lowered her gaze and frowned, raised her hand and turned the neck of her black baby-doll t-shirt inside out, looking at the label there. She smiled at it. "Can I see them again? It might help me believe that I'm not going crazy."

Her eyes crept to his shoulders and she let go of her t-shirt.

His wings?

They were aching to be free.

But he wasn't sure it was a good idea.

She had been gradually calming down since he had put his wings away. If he unfurled them, he could panic her again and undo any progress he had made with her. The soft look in her eyes pleaded him and he waged a war with himself, going in circles as he tried to decide what to do.

Let them out as she wanted? Or keep them hidden?

Hiding them left him feeling he wasn't being honest with her, that he was trying to be something else so she wouldn't run from him and would remain with him. He couldn't pretend to be just a man. As much as he wanted her to stay with him, he wouldn't be able to live with himself if it happened because he was masquerading as a man, a mortal.

He wanted her to accept him for what he was.

He wanted to be honest with her too and wanted to let everything be her decision, giving her the power she needed to make her feel comfortable and in control after he had tilted her world on its axis by revealing his kind to her.

If she believed that seeing his wings would help her come to terms with what he was, then he would let them out.

He nodded and she stepped back, as though afraid that he would knock her flying with them again. He wouldn't let that happen. This time he was ready and in control.

He wouldn't hurt her.

He would never hurt her ever again.

CHAPTER 5

Lukas moved away from Annelie anyway, finding space near the built-in wardrobes and the door to the bathroom. There was nothing there that he could knock over and Annelie was at a safe enough distance.

His shoulder blades itched, the skin shifting as his wings pushed for freedom.

He clenched his fists and let his white wings out as slowly as possible, so they didn't frighten Annelie.

Her gaze fixed on them as they appeared, no more than soft downy white feathers bunched at his shoulders at first. They grew larger, the bones growing and joints forming, until they were fully out. He spread them enough to get his feathers into line, not wanting to scare her with their size, and carefully furled them against his back. The long feathers tickled his bare legs, grazing his calves, and brushed his bottom.

He stood before her, naked, unashamed of both it and his wings.

This was who he was, and if she couldn't accept it, then perhaps it was for the best, even if it was breaking his heart.

"I wish I could have been honest with you," he whispered and her dark brown eyes moved from his wings to meet his green ones. "Everything has gone horribly wrong and I feel like crap. My head is killing me."

"Are you allowed to swear?" Her eyebrows rose.

He nodded. "I can do most things a human can without any repercussion."

She surprised him by stepping forwards and pressing her palm against his forehead. Her hand was cool, refreshing, and his eyes slipped shut. It felt so good to have her touch him, as though they had taken the first step towards moving past the fact that he was an angel.

"You'll feel better soon. You didn't look so good last night." Her voice was honey and sweetness to him, low spoken and filling him with soothing warmth. Her hand lingered against his brow. "I shouldn't have let you drink so much."

"I have never tasted alcohol before." The confession fell from his lips as a whisper as he absorbed the comfort of her touch, savoured it and tried to put to memory how it felt in case it never happened again.

"Really?" She tensed and he feared she would take her hand away. "I shouldn't have let you drink at all then. Will you get into trouble?"

He shrugged, opened his eyes and looked down into hers. "I would not consider it a perk of being banished. It is not as nice as mortals make it out to be."

"I could have told you that."

The intensity of her smile stole his breath together with the fact that her hand still rested against his forehead.

Was this progress?

She wasn't trying to run.

He had moved away from the door, giving her a clear path, and she had remained with him. She had chosen to touch him and be near him.

Was it possible that she could accept what he was and still love him?

He searched her eyes, hoping to find the answer there.

They softened, a touch of warmth igniting in them, and he lost himself in them and in her, was swept up in her before he even noticed what was happening.

She was so beautiful. He could look at her until the end of time and never tire. He had watched her age these past three years and she had only grown more beautiful to him. Her delicate features, large dark eyes and rosy sensual lips made her more stunning than any female he had ever seen, had kept her at the centre of his focus and always on his mind, even when he was away from her.

Annelie moved around him and he rolled his eyes closed when she ran a hand down his left wing. He held his groan inside, because he felt sure that if he let it out, if he revealed how deeply her caress affected him, she would run a mile.

The feel of her fingers stroking his feathers was divine.

"They're really real," she whispered and stopped behind him.

She ran her hands down both of his wings, teasing his feathers and his senses, stirring needs in him that he fought to deny as he wrestled for control over his body.

Images from last night danced through his mind, fuelling the wildfire building in his veins.

It had been everything that he had thought it would be and so much more. He had wanted to feel her hands on him, to kiss her and touch her, for so long now without truly realising it. He had thought it nothing more than lust, hunger brought about by years of celibacy, but it was more than that.

It was love.

The alcohol had done one good thing. It had cast his inhibitions aside and given him the courage to make a move on her. He could bear the pain in his head as payment for his glorious night with her.

He shivered when she caressed his lower back with long strokes of her fingers. Her touch was light, tickling, and he could sense concern in her again. It grew stronger as he focused on her, curiosity driving him to fix all of his senses on her so he could discover the source of that emotion.

What was she looking at that had her so worried?

"What happened?" Her fingertips traced another line across his back and then she stroked his shoulders.

The scars.

He hadn't realised that they were still there.

Was that what she had been touching this morning too? The thought that she would still lay her hands on him, would still feel such concern for him, added another slender thread to his hope, twining with the rest to make it stronger.

"I was punished." He couldn't bring himself to say any more, not when his throat closed and the memory of it made the scars on his back burn.

They had lashed him to remind him of his duty and the sin he had committed. *Sin.* He would have laughed at that if it hadn't hurt so much.

"But you said you didn't do it." She came around to stand in front of him, her dark brown eyes wide with confusion that he could easily feel in her as he focused on her, needing to fix his senses on something other than his back and his painful memories.

"I did not do it, but I cannot prove that. There is no evidence to the contrary. I have searched for it, returned to the scene of the crime every other night for the past three years trying to find a clue that would free me of my sin." Heaviness settled in his chest when he recalled how his hope had faded with each visit to the ruins of the building that remained in the closed lot. He shut his eyes as images of that night flashed across his mind and he could almost feel the heat of the blast, the sting of the cuts as he tumbled along the ground, and the smell of the fire. "I did not do it."

"Lukas?" Annelie's hand was soft against his cheek and, without thinking, he leaned into it, seeking the comfort she offered and taking it.

The memory faded again but it would return soon. It haunted him each night, filling his dreams with burning bodies and Heaven's Court and the look of shame on his fellow warriors' faces when the jury had passed judgement on him.

She murmured, "What happened?"

Did she really want to know?

He needed to see that she did. He needed to believe that someone was on his side and that if he told her everything, she would stand by him.

He looked deep into her eyes and used her hand against his face to strengthen the connection to her that had always been there. He couldn't usually feel humans' emotions so easily. Annelie's were always there for him to read though, held barely beneath the surface. She was so open with him and he cherished it, now more than ever.

He cleared his throat and steeled himself against the onslaught of his memories. He could relive them one more time for her, to tell her everything in the hope it would lift some of the burden from his heart and his shoulders. "There was going to be an event at a factory. My team received an order to go there. I was the first to arrive. When I did, the building exploded, incinerating everything. It transpired that no one knew of the event. It had not been foreseen."

"What does that mean?" Her hand remained against his face, lending him the strength to go on, to open himself to her.

He had been so ashamed when Heaven's Court had announced their verdict that he had shied away from his fellow warriors, had lived in solitude for the last three years, avoiding everyone he had once called friend, sure they wouldn't understand and would turn against him too.

She was the first person he had spoken with about what had happened, and part of him hoped that by speaking with her, he would find the courage and strength to face his friends and tell them too, and would find that they didn't turn their backs on him.

He wanted to believe the bond they shared ran deep enough to have them standing by his side too, fighting in his corner and believing him. Was it too much to ask? The bond he had formed with Apollyon, Einar and Rook had been powerful once, but was it powerful enough to make the two who remained, Apollyon and Einar, stand against Heaven for his sake?

"Only a supernatural creature can create an event that the Higher Order of Watchers wouldn't see." He tipped his head back, causing the tangled threads of his blond hair to fall back from his face, and sighed as he stared at the ceiling, imagining the blue vault beyond it and the white city beyond that. A place a small part of him still wanted to return to, even after what they had done to him. "An angel did it. They planted bombs and destroyed the building, with all of the humans still inside."

Was that angel still up there now, serving Heaven while he was living as an outcast in the mortal world?

Her eyes widened. "Why?"

"I do not know." He stepped back, clenched his fists and jaw as he dropped his head and stared hard at the wooden floor of his bedroom. "All I know is that I was there and no-one believes me when I say that I had been assigned to that area. The rest of my team did not receive the order, and there is no record of it. The records state that I was assigned somewhere else."

"Surely there has to be something you can do?"

Lukas laughed bitterly. "There was. I could appeal three years after being sentenced. I did and I failed... I accused my commander of falsifying the records to protect the perpetrator. Not my finest hour. The result is that I am stripped of my wings and most of my powers."

"Can't you appeal again?" Annelie sat on the end of the bed.

She seemed comfortable with his wings now, distracted by his plight, but he knew that it wasn't over. She still wasn't his.

Would she ever be?

He wasn't sure if she would be able to accept him as an angel. Could she accept him as a mortal? Was he brave enough to risk everything for her and her love?

He was the one unsure now. Heaven had turned its back on him but he wasn't brave enough to do the same to it. He still longed to clear his name and return to duty.

"No." He concentrated so his wings disappeared. He could still use a glamour but he preferred not to deceive Annelie by falsifying his appearance. When they were gone, he gathered his clothes and tugged on his boxer shorts and black jeans. "Well... I can when I have waited three hundred years."

She gasped, her eyes widening in horror as she looked at him. "That's ridiculous! What will you do?"

"Wait." What else could he do?

"You can't do that." She frowned at him, looking for all the world as if she thought him mad, or perhaps weak, for accepting his fate so easily. There was fight in her he had never noticed before, passion and courage that stirred his own, had foolish thoughts of doing something flowing through his mind. She shook her head, her scowl deepening. "There has to be some way of proving you're innocent."

The force behind those words convinced him that she believed he was as innocent as she said and that she wasn't going to walk out on him. She wanted to help him. It was written in every beautiful line of her face and the sharp, hard tone of her voice.

"Someone must have seen something." She leaned towards him, a flicker of despair crossing her features.

"They did, but Heaven's records don't show the angel involved. No one saw me or the real perpetrator. My kind are not recorded in Heaven's history of Earth. They only saw the explosion happen and then I returned and reported it, incriminating myself." Lukas paused and frowned. Why hadn't he thought of it earlier? "Heaven's records may not record angels but Hell's might."

"Hell?" Annelie looked even more uncertain now. "What are you going to do, walk in there and ask the Devil if he'll take a look for you? I went to Sunday School and I know that he probably won't help an angel, even a fellow fallen one."

She bit her lip when his gaze snapped to her, an explosive combination of dismay, shock and anger detonating inside him to rock him to his core. She dropped her chin and her cheeks coloured deeply as her shame and guilt swept over him.

He might have fallen but he wasn't the Devil.

She peered up at him through the messy strands of red hair that had escaped her ponytail, her apology in her eyes, and Lukas sighed and reined in his temper, refusing to let it control him.

He knew she hadn't meant it like that, but being compared to the Devil had struck a chord deep within him, one that had his hope fading fast as he stared down at her.

He would never survive three hundred years on Earth waiting for his appeal.

He wasn't strong enough to endure such endless pain, not without succumbing to temptation as the Devil had. He had to do something about it, just as Annelie had said. He couldn't appeal to Heaven again, but there was another way he could clear his name and he didn't need to go to Heaven in order to make it happen.

He needed to go to Hell.

"I do not need to ask the Devil. There is an angel who will likely help me." Lukas sat beside her on the bed. "Annelie?"

She turned to face him, her eyes meeting his and her expression soft and inviting.

He hesitated. Was he strong enough to say what was on the tip of his tongue? Would she agree or would she leave him? He was moving too fast but he couldn't go without her. He had to take the risk and believe that she wanted to give him a chance, and that she would say yes.

"Will you come to Paris with me?" It was one of the most difficult questions he had ever asked. He waited with bated breath, desperate to hear her answer. When she said nothing, just stared at him, he leaned closer to her and resisted the temptation to take hold of her hand. "Please? Give me time to prove to you that it doesn't matter that I am an angel... that I am still the man you have known these past three years."

She still hesitated.

Lukas swallowed and took hold of her hand, clutching it in both of his, caressing the back with his thumbs. She had to agree. She had to come with him and give him a second chance. He couldn't do this without her and he couldn't leave her here. If he did that, he was sure he would never see her again.

"Annelie?" He was pressing her, he knew that, but he needed her.

She finally nodded.

Lukas smiled as relief swept through him, loosening his tight muscles and lifting some of the weight from his shoulders. "We shall get you some things from your home and then fly straight there."

"I thought you couldn't fly?" Her brow crinkled in confusion.

His face fell and all of the weight that had lifted from his shoulders dropped back onto them. This punishment was going to take some getting used to. Even a mention of the fact that he was unable to fly had him aching inside, slipping into a dark place where he feared the Devil would easily be able to sway him to his side.

"By plane then," he whispered and thought about how difficult it was going to be to travel via human methods. "Do you have an old passport?"

She stared at him, her expression distant, as though she wasn't quite keeping up with him and everything was sweeping her along. He waited for her to catch up, because he had pressed her enough for one day. Rushing her now would only make her change her mind.

She glanced at his shoulders and then finally nodded again. "What use is that though?"

"I can alter it but we will have to get tickets at the airport so I can be near the terminal to change it there too. I still have that power." Lukas stared at his bare feet.

He would have to get used to seeing floors and pavements. He didn't think he could bring himself to see the day sky until all this was over and he had proven his innocence. He would do it somehow. He would end this punishment and free himself by making them see they had the wrong angel.

He had always put humans before him. He had never harmed them.

He just needed to get to Paris and speak with Apollyon, and convince the angel to give him access to Hell. Paris was only a few hours from London by plane. There was a chance that by tonight he could have the proof he needed to clear his name.

He closed his eyes.

Flying was going to be torture. Even if he didn't look, he would know that he was high in the sky, where he longed to be. He would endure it though. He would find the strength to bear the pain of flying without using his own wings.

Annelie's hand came to rest against his shoulder, warm against his bare skin. "Why don't we take the train? I've never been through the tunnel before. It'll be much more fun than flying and will give us time to talk."

Lukas smiled, placed his hand over hers and squeezed it, silently thanking her. It was kind of her to pretend that she hadn't noticed his pain. It was kind of her to see the suffering his loss of flying caused him and to understand it.

Perhaps there was hope for him. For them.

He would do everything in his power to make things right.

He would prove his innocence.

He would prove his love for her.

CHAPTER 6

Annelie still couldn't quite believe it.

Lukas was an angel.

It seemed so impossible, even when she had seen his wings.

She had done more than merely see them. She had touched them. They had been soft, tickling her fingertips, and sturdy where they connected to his back, strong and powerful. She had touched them but it all still felt unreal, as if she had dreamed them.

Her gaze kept gravitating towards him, even when she knew that she should be making the most of her surroundings. She had never been to Paris, had always wanted to see it, but now that she was here she couldn't take her eyes off Lukas.

He was gorgeous as he walked beside her down the elegant shopping street, dressed in a white linen shirt and blue jeans suited to the warm weather, the finger-length strands of his fair hair tousled and wild.

Her mind flashed back to how he had looked sleeping next to her, sated from their lovemaking and lost in deep dreams. His hair had been messy then, and every time she looked at him, she remembered how incredible it had felt to be with him.

He was right about her.

The revelation that he was an angel hadn't changed her feelings for him but it had changed something. It stood before her, undeniable, a hurdle that she felt she would never get over. She wasn't sure if she would ever be able to accept it.

How was she supposed to love an angel?

It felt so impossible.

Lukas's green gaze shifted to her, captivating her and making her heart beat faster. She still loved him though and there was so much hurt in his eyes, and he had endured so much suffering, that he at least deserved her to try.

And she would.

She would give it her all and not only for his sake. She was doing this for hers too, because part of her still wanted to be with him. She wanted to accept him for what he was. She just wasn't sure whether she would be able to do it. Without his wings, he looked like the man she had known for the last three years, and it was easy to fool herself into thinking she had dreamed he was an angel and he was really just a man like any of the others passing them on the tree-lined avenue.

She needed to see him as an angel again. It was the only way it was going to sink in that he was one, that he wasn't like her or the men around her. He was something else.

"Do you know where we're going?" She smiled and relief lit his eyes again.

It bloomed there whenever she dared to smile or let her guard down and showed him a hint of affection. It warmed her whenever she saw it and knew that she had caused it. She had eased his pain a little.

She couldn't comprehend how painful it must have been for him to be accused of something as terrible as the deaths of one hundred people, but she could see it in him. He bore it well, and abided the rules of his punishment.

He had confessed on the train that while he wasn't allowed to fly, he could still do it. He could have flown them to Paris but he hadn't.

If he had committed the crime, he wouldn't have cared about breaking the rules. He would have flown. Her heart said that he was innocent and she believed it, and in him. She didn't know what help she could be, but she wanted to be with him and give him all the support he needed. She wanted to help in some small way, and if she happened to get over the fact that the gorgeous man walking beside her was an angel at the same time, well, she wasn't going to complain.

"Not really." A brief smile tugged at his lips and he stopped in the street, took hold of her arm, and led her over to the buildings, away from the crowd walking along the Champs Elysees.

The golden stone buildings shadowed them, keeping the hot summer sun at bay and giving her a little relief from the heat. She shouldn't have chosen to wear her usual black jeans and t-shirt. She thought about the clothes she had packed in her small backpack and sighed. They were all jeans and t-shirts or shirts. She should have packed at least one dress. They had been in such a hurry that she hadn't thought about the weather.

After calling Andy and telling him to take care of the pub for a few days, she had rushed to the Eurostar terminal with Lukas. They had managed to get tickets on the next train. Lukas had changed her old passport somehow and the computer system too, just as he had said he would. She still wasn't sure how he had done it but she had decided it was some sort of magic.

They had arrived early in the afternoon and had been walking around Paris ever since. Annelie had caught glimpses of the Eiffel Tower, the Arc de Triomphe, and the river Seine, but most of the time she had been watching Lukas.

He hadn't once looked at the sky.

It was a beautiful blue canvas above them, cloudless and endless.

Would it pain him to see it?

Annelie had seen his hurt back in his bedroom when he had mentioned flying. She hadn't lied. She had always wanted to come to Paris through the Channel Tunnel, but in part her decision had been because of the pain she had seen in him. She didn't want him to suffer because of someone else. Whoever had done this, committed the crime in the first place and set Lukas up to take the fall for them, was going to pay and she wasn't going to let it hurt him anymore.

"Can you find them?" Annelie studied his handsome face, taking in how good he looked in daylight.

She had never seen him in natural light before. Even in the shadows, he looked different. It wasn't just the change in clothes. There was a light in his green eyes, warmth that stole her breath whenever he looked at her and made her believe that he was telling the truth about his feelings too.

He nodded, lifted his hand and swept a rogue strand of hair from his face, preening it back as he looked around them at the stream of people flowing along the busy shopping street, and then back at her.

She frowned when he closed his eyes and took a deep breath.

Stood like a statue for at least a minute.

She waited for him to open his eyes again and relax, growing aware of everyone glancing at them as they passed. When he remained stood still with his eyes closed, she couldn't stop hers from drifting over him. Damn, he did look good, and too human. He was making it hard to remember that he was an angel, her eyes beginning to trick her mind and her heart into believing he was just another gorgeous man.

He wasn't though, and whenever she thought she was making progress with comprehending that and finding some balance in the midst of her turbulent feelings, it came back and smacked her straight between the eyes.

Angels existed.

And Lukas was one of them.

With or without the wings on show, he was an angel, straight out of Heaven. It was no use denying it.

Whenever she remembered it, whenever it hit her again and she looked at him with clear eyes, she found herself faltering. She didn't know what she felt for him in those moments, or whether she should feel anything at all. He was something else, something supernatural, and she was mortal.

They didn't belong together.

She idly touched the point over her heart.

No matter how much she felt they did.

He finally opened his eyes and looked back into hers.

"This way." He took hold of her hand and she stared down at his as they walked along the street, weaving through the people.

His grip on her was tight, strong, and she remembered how wonderful his hands had felt on her body. The memory of last night chased away her confusion, clearing her head of her muddled emotions, and warmed her from the inside, starting a fire in her veins that quickly spread throughout her entire body until she burned to have his hands on her again, moulding and caressing her, teasing her body to the point of torture.

It had been incredible, exciting, and she didn't regret what she had done with him.

Nothing was going to change that, and nothing would change her attraction to him, but the knowledge that Lukas was an angel still hung between them and what little bravery she'd had around him had disappeared because of it.

She wished she were strong enough to throw aside her fears, and embrace Lukas and her feelings for him, uncaring of the fact he was an angel, but she wasn't. It was a leap that she had tried to take several times in their journey to Paris, and she had always frozen and found a reason not to go through with it.

What was she afraid of? That Heaven would somehow punish her?

It hadn't punished her for sleeping with Lukas before she had known he was an angel, so why would it do so if she slept with him again? Why would it punish her if she dragged her courage up from her toes and told him that she still had feelings for him?

It hadn't reprimanded Lukas either, and he had spoken about the rules of his kind in a way that made her feel as though they still applied to him, even though he was fallen.

Was it really alright for them to love each other?

Annelie's gaze drifted up to the sky. She wished she could ask someone up there. Maybe if she could speak to someone other than Lukas about this, she would be able to get her head on straight.

Would the angel that Lukas was going to meet answer her questions for her and help her gain some perspective? She hoped they would.

Lukas looked over his shoulder at her, his eyes dark and pupils wide. She shivered when he raked his gaze down her, hungry and full of desire, sparking her own lustful thoughts about him. She shouldn't be thinking such things. He was an angel. No matter what he said, she was sure it was a sin. No matter how much she craved him, she had to resist.

His deep green eyes promised her all the sin she wanted and all the passion she craved.

She looked away and then in front of her when Lukas led her around a corner at the end of the Champs Elysees near the Arc de Triomphe. It towered before her, a beautiful golden stone arch that lived up to its name. It was triumphant, powerful, and bigger than she had expected.

"There." Lukas pointed to the top and tugged on her hand.

They hurried across the busy road that circled the arch, waited in the line and then went in, climbing the winding staircase.

The person he knew lived here?

Her legs were aching when they reached the top and stepped out into the sunlight.

Annelie stopped, her breath rushing from her as she lifted her head and the view hit her hard.

It was incredible.

The whole of Paris stretched before her, the avenues that surrounded the arch leading her eyes in different directions like the points of a compass. In the distance, the Eiffel Tower shimmered in the heat haze, beautiful and like something out of a dream.

She walked forwards, bringing Lukas with her now, and found a space between some people at the wall.

She stopped there and stared, trying to take it all in. She had never seen anything so beautiful and fascinating. She could see right down the length of the Champs Elysees to the square and Egyptian column at the other end.

Lukas stepped up beside her, close enough that his body brushed hers, and placed his hand beside her free one on the cream stone wall in front of her. Annelie shifted her hand, her heart trembling in her throat, until her little finger touched his thumb.

His chest pressed against her arm and side and the world went out of focus, drifting away at the feel of him near to her. She wasn't afraid and she wasn't going to move away. She liked the feel of him against her. She felt safe and warm, loved and protected. She had been dying for him to touch her all day, to brave something that she couldn't, and he had finally taken the leap.

She couldn't deny him his reward.

Not when she was enjoying it so much.

She frowned when he stepped away from her. When she turned to see why he had moved, a strong wind gusted against her, causing her red hair to stream out behind her and tangle. She raised her hand to shield her eyes from the sun and the wind, and squinted as dust blew at her and Lukas held her hand more tightly.

Her eyes widened and she swallowed when she saw what was causing the sudden breeze.

A black-winged angel was descending towards them.

She glanced around at the tourists, panic lighting up her veins and pushing her to run as they probably were.

Only none of the other humans around her seemed to notice him. They continued talking and laughing, enjoying the view of the city as if nothing strange was happening, as if there wasn't a dark angel about to land on the roof of the arch right in front of them.

Her heart thundered and she stepped closer to Lukas.

If Lukas was here to meet this man, then she could easily believe that he could take Lukas into Hell. He looked like the Devil, and like a warrior, his powerful body clad in obsidian armour edged with gold that protected his chest, forearms, hips and shins. His huge dark wings beat the hot air at her as he hovered above the ground, blue eyes scrutinising her as she tucked closer to Lukas and the wind causing his black ponytail to flutter across his broad shoulders.

Perhaps she wouldn't ask him about angels and relationships after all. He didn't look like the sort of man she could speak to about such things.

Lukas placed his arm around her shoulders, drawing her closer, and she was thankful for it as just his touch calmed her nerves enough that the urge to flee faded. Would he protect her from this man?

She felt as though she needed him to.

The angel finally landed and walked towards her, each step cranking her nerves back up again until she felt tight inside, on the verge of wanting to run again. Thoughts of getting the hell away from him drifted into the background as his appearance changed before her eyes, his black wings disappearing and a sharp black suit replacing his armour. Magic. Angels could perform magic.

He smiled wickedly when he stopped close to them, his blue eyes sparkling with it.

"She is not gifted, and I was invisible to mortal eyes, and yet she saw me, which means that you let her see." The man's deep voice spoke of amusement as his gaze drifted to Lukas's hand where they touched.

"She knows of us. I thought it was best she see you for what you are." Lukas released her shoulders and took hold of her hand again. "It has been a long time, Apollyon."

"It has, Lukas. I was surprised, but pleased to hear your call. What brings you to Paris? Romance?" Apollyon's blue gaze slid to her and he grinned. Annelie swallowed and her heartbeat quickened. Romance? The way he had said it hadn't sounded teasing. Perhaps he was being serious and such a thing was possible between angels and mortals. "And does she have a name?"

"Annelie," Lukas said before she could utter it and she smiled shakily when the dark angel glanced her way again before settling his gaze back on Lukas as he cleared his throat. "And I am here to ask a favour of you."

"Then we should go somewhere more private." Apollyon looked skyward. "We will fly to my place here."

"No." Annelie jerked forwards and his blue eyes dropped to her. He raised a single black eyebrow. Her voice trembled. "I don't think we should fly. It's such a nice day and I've never been to Paris. Couldn't we walk?"

Lukas looked at her as though she was the angel for making such a suggestion.

She did want to walk but she had mostly done it to protect him and save him from having to explain the terrible situation he was in to his friend. She was sure that Apollyon knew of Lukas's plight, but something told her that Lukas had kept his recent failed appeal to himself. His friend wouldn't have mentioned flying if he knew.

"As the lady wishes." Apollyon nodded and then held his hand out, motioning to the exit.

Did they have to go right now? She wanted to stay a little longer and take in her surroundings.

She glanced around at the panorama of rooftops and the Eiffel Tower and then conceded. They weren't here as tourists. Lukas needed help and she had to place him and his feelings first. He had asked her to come with him so she had time to overcome her confusion about him and so he could somehow find a way to prove his innocence, not so he could romance her in the beautiful city.

Wait. Did she want to be romanced?

She shifted her gaze to Lukas, and when his eyes slid to meet hers and warmth spread through her, she realised that she did. She wanted Lukas to romance her, to convince her that what they shared was allowed and that it was fine to be with him. It was *right* to be with him.

Lukas squeezed her hand.

She nodded and followed Apollyon towards the exit. When they reached the stairs, Lukas released her hand and went before her.

Annelie's gaze settled on his backpack and then dropped to his hand as she followed the spiral staircase back down. It had felt nice to have him holding hers. Everything had been starting to feel normal until Apollyon had flown in. Even then, the sight of him hadn't shocked her as she had expected it to. Seeing him flying towards them had seemed perfectly natural, as though she had known all her life that angels existed rather than just the past day.

If she saw Lukas's wings again, would she feel different now? The first time had frightened her, and the second time had still been strange. If she saw them again, would she just see them as normal? Was it really so easy to accept the presence of angels in the world and grow used to them?

Neither of the men in front of her scared her. Not even the thought that they had confirmed the existence of God and the Devil was shocking anymore. It all seemed so normal, and she felt as though she had been spending the past few hours trying to convince herself that it wasn't. Maybe it was time she gave up the fight and went with the flow, and saw where it took her.

Lukas looked back at her, his green eyes meeting hers, a question shining in them. She smiled, showing him that she was alright.

She really was alright.

It was incredible to think that she had adjusted so quickly to what he was. The revelation caused some of her fear and confusion to fade, leaving a feeling close to peace inside her that opened up her mind to all the questions that had been lurking at the back of it.

Apollyon had changed his appearance and had mentioned being invisible when flying. Did Lukas have such powers? He had changed the passport. Could he be invisible and change his appearance too? Not even that would shock her now.

Was it this magic that made his wings disappear? Apollyon's had disappeared in a flash but Lukas's had slowly shrunk into his back. Did Apollyon use a different method to hide them?

She wanted to ask but didn't want to disturb them. They were talking as they walked, speaking low enough that she couldn't quite make out what they were saying, and she felt left out, stuck at the back, playing the fifth wheel.

When they stepped out onto the street, Lukas dropped back to be beside her again and Apollyon walked on the other side of him. They continued to talk but Lukas glanced at her every so often, as though he was trying to include her. Her questions burned on the tip of her tongue and she was sure that Lukas would answer them for her and that this was the reason he had brought her along, so she could learn more about him and accept him for what he was.

She just needed to find that courage that had bloomed inside her last night and use it again.

Annelie cleared her throat and touched his hand.

Lukas looked over at her and slowed down, earning glares from the people walking the Champs Elysees for getting in their way. Apollyon frowned at her too and she clammed up, her question fleeing under his scrutiny. Clearly she was interrupting.

The way Lukas looked at her, warmth in his green eyes that offered comfort and encouragement, told her that he didn't care. He wanted her to speak with him, wanted her to ask whatever was on her mind. She didn't need to hold back with him.

"Are you alright?" Lukas took hold of her hand, his fingers light against hers, and brushed his thumb across her knuckles.

"What powers do you have? I mean... his wings just disappeared but yours..." Her nerve failed and she looked away so she couldn't see Apollyon staring at her and cursed herself as her courage failed her again.

She blew out her breath.

She was stronger than this.

She had questions and she wanted answers, and she was damn well going to get them.

Lukas moved to stand in front of her, blocking her view of the other angel, and smiled. "He is using a sort of spell to make him appear as though he is wearing a suit and has no wings. If he lifted the glamour, you would see wings again and what he is really wearing."

"Armour." She peered past Lukas to Apollyon.

She preferred him in a suit.

The gold-edged black breastplate, arm and shin guards had been too dark and menacing, and definitely too revealing. Other than those three items, he had only been wearing pointed strips of armour over his hips that left little to the imagination.

Did Lukas own such armour? She pictured him in it and almost smiled to herself. Lukas would look gorgeous in such a thing, even more tempting than he was now.

She shook the image away and met his gaze as it drilled into her and she sensed he was waiting. "And when your wings disappear?"

"Lukas is being kind to you." Apollyon stepped up beside him, slightly taller and almost as handsome.

He had an air of death and sin about him though, and she didn't like it. She preferred the way Lukas looked. Kind and warm but definitely sensual and passionate, with a mouth made for kissing.

Apollyon arched an eyebrow at Lukas. "For some reason, Lukas isn't fooling your eyes. He has made his wings disappear. It is difficult, painful and requires great concentration. His appearance to you is real."

She hadn't realised that it hurt Lukas to hide his wings.

Why didn't he use magic as Apollyon did?

She looked into his eyes and saw the answer there.

It was more than kindness to her. He had said that he hated lying to her. Did he view changing his appearance with a spell as that? She supposed it was in a way. He had hidden his wings and dressed in mortal clothes every time he had come out to see her at the pub. He had put himself through pain in order not to lie to her. He could have taken the easy route but he had done what he believed was the right thing, regardless of whether it hurt.

Because he loved her.

It warmed her and she smiled into his eyes, silently thanking him for being so honest with her and going to such great lengths to remain that way.

"I don't mind if you use a spell instead." She curled her fingers around his, nerves fluttering in her chest and belly as she lightly gripped his hand, silently showing him that she was growing more comfortable around him.

His green eyes softened as they fell to their joined hands, a glimmer of relief in them that warmed her.

He met her offer with a shake of his head. "I prefer it this way."

"You are lucky you have a choice." Apollyon gave Lukas a tight-lipped smile. "I have no choice but to hide them physically when Serenity desires them gone. The downside to loving a witch."

Annelie's eyes widened. Witch? That did shock her. Witches existed. What else was out there that had previously been nothing but fantasy to her? Demons? Vampires? Werewolves?

"How is Serenity?" Lukas slipped his fingers between Annelie's and chased away her thoughts of horror film monsters, bringing her focus back to him.

Apollyon sighed and smiled, and although he was clearly trying to sound put out, there was so much affection in his blue eyes that they looked brighter, almost matching the sky stretching above them.

"Eager to meet you since I mentioned your call. Of course, she will be even happier when she sees that you have female company." Apollyon's gaze landed on Annelie for a moment and then he started walking.

Annelie walked with them, lost in her thoughts, listening to Lukas and Apollyon's conversation about Serenity, living in Paris, and the things they had been up to since last speaking with each other.

Apollyon was in love with a witch.

Her gaze traced Lukas's profile.

If Apollyon and Serenity lived together, which she suspected they did, then Lukas had been telling her the truth. It wasn't a sin for him to love a mortal or for her to love him. She could be with him if she wanted it.

But she still wasn't sure.

She was sure of something though.

She was going to ask Serenity all about her relationship with Apollyon. It had to be part of the reason that Lukas had made her come with him. It wasn't just about spending time with him and asking him questions.

He had brought her here to meet Serenity.

He wanted her to see that it was possible for a mortal to love an angel and be with them.

She glanced at Lukas again.

She was beginning to feel that it was.

CHAPTER 7

Apollyon warmed to her throughout the long walk, beginning to include her in the conversation and even going as far as teasing Lukas about things. Lukas didn't rise to the bait and quickly ended the conversation whenever Apollyon mentioned their relationship. After the third mention, Lukas said that it was complicated and a knowing look graced Apollyon's handsome face.

Annelie's feet were tired and sore by the time they reached the residential area and the apartment.

Apollyon stared up the height of the elegant building. "Top floor."

Why didn't that surprise her? Lukas's apartment had been at the top of his building too, and she supposed it made sense that an angel would want to live high up in the sky.

Apollyon's beautiful white townhouse stood on a leafy avenue that made her a little jealous. Her place in the suburbs of London looked shabby and dark in comparison. Even Lukas's beautiful apartment put it to shame.

Were all angels loaded?

Did they even get paid?

It seemed a bit wrong that they might be, but if they were living on Earth they would need some means by which to pay for things and a roof over their heads.

Annelie puffed her way up the stairs to the top floor of the building, trailing behind Lukas and Apollyon, slowing down with each step. She swore they were never-ending. Her feet were throbbing as they finally hit the top of the building, and she remained a step behind Lukas while Apollyon opened the black door to his apartment.

The moment it opened, a petite blonde woman in tight blue jeans and a white camisole top was in his arms.

He smiled, wrapped his arms around her and pressed a kiss to her hair.

He said something in French and Serenity came out of his arms and looked at Lukas with wide hazel eyes. She spoke in French to him, rapidly enough that Annelie didn't catch a word of it, and Lukas replied.

Fluently.

Dismay crashed over Annelie.

She had failed French in school. Her ability with it went as far as the obligatory please, thank you, getting the bill and ordering coffee. Even that was sketchy now, and she struggled to remember what she had learned all those years ago.

For a moment, she wished that she hadn't come, because she sure that she was going to make a complete idiot of herself and she didn't want to appear unschooled or stupid, but then Lukas's green eyes captured hers and her fear melted away.

"This is Annelie." He held his hand out to her and she shakily placed hers into it, hiding none of her nerves from him.

He drew her close to him and calm washed through her as his masculine scent and heat swirled around her and his grip on her hand grew firmer, more possessive, and maybe a little protective too. There was love in his touch, comfort he offered to her and she gladly accepted, strength no man had ever given to her before. It told her that he was there with her, for her, and that he wouldn't let anything bad happen to her. He would take care of her, if only she would let him.

This time, she wasn't going to fight him on it. She stole all the strength and courage he offered, badly needing it as she looked at Serenity.

Annelie was about to say that she didn't speak French when she was suddenly in Serenity's arms, being hugged so tightly it was hard to breathe.

"He did not say... company was coming... no... that..." Serenity released her and frowned. Guilt churned Annelie's stomach as Serenity struggled with English when she hadn't even attempted to speak French. "Lukas had a friend."

Serenity's smile was dazzling. Apollyon grinned, threw his arm around her shoulders, and pulled her against him. Her smile widened when she looked up at him.

"You speak terrible English." His smile turned playful.

"I am warming up." Serenity frowned and slapped his chest.

"It's better than my French." Annelie shrank against Lukas when they all looked at her, her confidence wavering again as she waited for them to judge her. "Unless our conversation is going to be strictly ordering coffee or pleasantries."

Lukas laughed and it warmed her to hear it. "Coffee is not such a good thing for us."

Apollyon grinned. Serenity blushed.

Annelie had the feeling she was missing something.

Serenity took her arm, stealing her away from Lukas, and led her into the bright spacious apartment.

"It is like... *Viagra*," Serenity whispered when they were distant from Lukas and Apollyon.

"Oh." Annelie blushed at the thought and removed her backpack.

Lukas definitely didn't need that, and something about Serenity's smile said that Apollyon didn't either.

"How long?" Serenity released her arm and went into a large beech wood kitchen. She looked back at Annelie, concentration etched on her face. "I mean... you have been together how long?"

"We're not exactly together." Annelie placed her backpack down on the tiled floor, leaned against the counter and looked over her shoulder, afraid that Lukas and Apollyon were going to follow them.

What were they talking about in the living room?

She could see them through the door and they looked deep in conversation, both of them frowning as they sat on the beige couches that formed an L in the bright white room.

Was Lukas telling him about his appeal and what had happened? She felt as though she should be with him, giving him support, not idly talking in the kitchen.

Lukas dumped his backpack by his feet, glanced over at her and smiled. She motioned towards herself and then him and he shook his head and waved a hand at her. She took that to mean for her to talk to Serenity. Perhaps it was best to give him time to talk business with Apollyon, and there was a lot she wanted to ask Serenity.

The petite witch was her best chance for getting answers.

Far better than asking Apollyon.

"I only just found out that he's an angel." Annelie tore her eyes away from him. "How was it for you when you realised?"

"They're angels?" Serenity gasped and then smiled, her English improving every second and making Annelie feel terrible for not being able to speak French. "I have known all my life they exist."

Annelie snuck a glance at Lukas.

He was watching her and she smiled at the same time as he did. His head tilted and his gaze slowly dropped to her body, raked over her curves and set her on fire again. He definitely didn't need coffee to get him going, and at this point, she didn't either. She kept telling herself to keep her distance until she had figured out what she was going to do but her heart wasn't listening, and neither was her body. She still wanted him. Burned for him.

"Would you like a drink? I have English tea."

"That would be lovely." Annelie dragged her attention back to Serenity.

She couldn't speak French, but she could at least be courteous to her hostess by listening to her and enjoying her company. Although, it was hard to keep her focus away from Lukas.

She caught snippets of Lukas's conversation while Serenity made a pot of tea. He was telling Apollyon about what had happened to him, and by the sounds of things, this was the first time Apollyon was hearing about it. Why hadn't Lukas told his friend about things earlier?

It had taken him a lot of effort to tell her. She tried to put herself in his shoes and imagine what she would have felt like if she had been wrongly accused of a heinous crime, of committing something that so clearly went against everything she stood for and believed in, and against her very nature. It would have devastated her, but it would have made her feel ashamed too. Had shame kept Lukas from telling Apollyon what had happened to him?

She glanced at him again, her eyebrows furrowing and heart aching for him as a myriad of emotions crossed his face as they talked, every one of them laced with pain. Apollyon offered him a warm smile and placed his hand on Lukas's knee, squeezed it in a way that had Lukas smiling tightly and nodding, and his mood lifting a little, some of the sombreness disappearing from his eyes.

"I have witnessed angels in the pool in Hell." Apollyon took his hand back and rubbed his lower lip, a thoughtful furrow to his brow as he leaned back into the couch.

Lukas looked pleased to hear that.

She smiled at how happy he seemed. There was hope in his expression again and she was glad to see it, was so focused on him that she missed what he said. When Apollyon next spoke, he mentioned her name.

She wanted to keep listening to hear what Lukas would say about her, but Serenity stole her attention away from them.

"Would you like tea outside?" Serenity placed the pot and cups onto a tray with some small pastries, and as much as Annelie wanted to ask her to wait so she could hear what the men were saying about her, she smiled and nodded.

It was rude to eavesdrop anyway.

It didn't stop her from casting a glance back at Lukas as she followed Serenity.

He looked tense again, but there was heat in his eyes, warmth that beckoned her as he flicked a glance her way and then focused back on Apollyon. She could easily interpret that look, knew without hearing what he was saying that he was talking about her, and thinking about what they had shared last night.

That had her thinking about it too, lost in memories of their moment together, so much so she tripped on the doorstep and barely caught herself on the table as she stumbled onto a large rooftop patio.

"Are you alright?" Serenity's hazel eyes flooded with concern.

Annelie smiled and shook her head. "I'm fine. Just clumsy."

"Clumsy is… my middle name." The blonde smiled warmly at her and Annelie had the feeling she was telling the truth when she said, "I can be a little chaotic."

"You have a beautiful home." She stared out at the view of the wide but quiet car-lined road below the railing across the front of the terrace and the leafy park beyond it, feeling even more as though she lived in a hovel.

Serenity's smile widened as she set the tray down on the elegant green cast iron table. "It was not always this way. I had a very petite place once. Apollyon has big tastes."

Annelie nodded. Having seen Lukas's apartment, she could easily believe it was Apollyon's decision to live in such a place. She sat down opposite Serenity and thought everything over as Serenity tied her long blonde hair up and then poured the tea.

"I wore that look once." Serenity offered her the cup.

Annelie took it and added a little milk and sugar. "What look?"

"The one that says you do not believe an angel can love." Serenity placed a pastry on a small plate and set it down in front of Annelie. She smiled knowingly. "He will make you see otherwise."

"Did Apollyon change your mind?" Her pulse quickened and she fought her rising nerves, tried to settle back into the chair with her tea but couldn't relax as she waited for Serenity to answer.

It felt as if everything hinged on this conversation with the witch, as if this was the moment that would either free her from the doubts and fears that plagued her, or have her leaving and breaking her own heart in the process.

"My dark angel?" Serenity's smile widened, a wistful look entering her eyes as she stared off into the distance. "He is… how do you say… very persuasive. I was unsure, like you… but many angels love mortals. It is their choice."

Annelie was starting to believe that. If she wanted it, she could be with Lukas. She did want it, but she was still scared of reaching out and taking it. She sipped her tea and then sighed as her stomach twisted in knots, her heart going in circles.

"He is sweet on you, non?" Serenity stirred her tea and looked past Annelie to the open glass doors behind her. "He is nice. He has a good aura."

"Apollyon said you were a witch." Annelie took another sip of her tea. "Can you feel things about Lukas?"

"He will not hurt you... if that is your fear." Serenity leaned back into her chair and smiled, the beautiful green park as her backdrop. "I thought it too, that I would have my heart broken, but a year has gone and I am still crazy for him, and I think he is crazy for me."

Annelie could believe that too.

The way Apollyon had held Serenity, had carefully kissed her, and the love that had been in his eyes, all of it spoke to Annelie and was another step towards convincing her to give things with Lukas a chance.

"Do you love Lukas?"

That question hung in the air, gently spoken but filling her with tension as she pondered the answer.

Annelie frowned at her tea and studied her feelings. They clouded, mixing together until she was no longer certain. Doubts about Lukas still lingered, along with thoughts about him being an angel and a sliver of belief that he couldn't love her, a mortal. She sighed and focused on her feelings, piecing together the positive ones and discarding her fears until her head was clear again.

"I don't know. I think I do." Annelie paused. What was she saying? She had been sure of her feelings before Lukas had revealed that he was an angel, and even after that she had known several times that her feelings for him were unchanged. She still loved him. "I do."

"That is all you need then. Love. Look past the wings to the man and his heart. Lukas must love you. He worries. I feel it." Serenity looked beyond her again, her gaze losing focus and her voice growing distant. "He worries you will leave and has brought you here so you will not. They are not as strong as they appear... men in love."

Annelie felt the truth in those words.

Lukas did love her and he wasn't the only one who was afraid. She was scared too, afraid that he would leave her or that things wouldn't work. Serenity had known the same fear that gripped her but she had taken the leap and she looked so happy. Annelie wanted that too. She wanted to love Lukas and see past the wings to the man beneath. She wanted to be with him. She wanted what Serenity and Apollyon had.

"What are you two conspiring about?" That deep voice coming from behind her made Annelie jump and she gasped as her tea spilled on her jeans, scalding her thigh.

Serenity said something in rapid French that earned Annelie an apologetic look from Apollyon. He pulled a cloth out of thin air and offered it to her. Annelie went to take it but Lukas beat her to it, snatching it from his friend and coming to crouch before her.

He carefully dabbed the wet patch on her legs.

"Does it hurt?" The look in his green eyes was beautiful, exactly what she had needed to reassure her that she was making the right decision.

There was such warmth and love in them, concern that touched her heart. She shook her head and placed her hand over his. His gaze dropped there and he stared at their joined hands for a moment and then into her eyes.

She smiled.

He smiled right back at her.

"Tell me we do not look so sappy." Apollyon caught Serenity around the waist and she shrieked when he swept her up into his arms, turning with her.

"Not at all. You look particularly manly like that." Lukas stood and the cloth disappeared from his hand.

Apollyon scowled and set Serenity down.

"What were you two conspiring about?" Annelie turned Apollyon's question against him and Lukas.

"Hell." Lukas's look darkened. "We will go tomorrow. Apollyon believes we may find what I am looking for in the history recorded there."

Serenity's face blanched and her gaze darted to Apollyon. Annelie suddenly wished she knew French because that look unnerved her and she didn't understand a word Serenity said as she began talking to him. Apollyon spoke back to her and their conversation turned heated as she responded, her face darkening as she planted her hands on her hips.

Serenity shook her head and threw Apollyon's hand aside when he tried to touch her. She pointed at Lukas and Annelie looked at him. What was the problem?

Apollyon held his hands out, his tone turning soothing, and smiled.

It didn't stop Serenity from frowning at him.

He caught Serenity's hand and didn't let go this time when she slapped at his wrist and fingers. He tugged her to him, wrapped his arms around her, and whispered something against her fair hair. It seemed to calm Serenity but did nothing to settle Annelie's nerves.

What was going on?

She looked at Lukas for an explanation.

"It is dangerous to enter Hell." It was all the reason he needed to give her.

A chill tumbled down her spine and she suddenly understood why Serenity wasn't happy.

His grave tone and sombre expression said it wasn't merely a little dangerous for him to enter Hell. It was extremely dangerous. Life or death dangerous.

She didn't want Lukas to get hurt. He needed to do this to prove his innocence, but she didn't want to lose him and she feared that if she let him go, she would never see him again. Wasn't there another way he could get the proof he needed?

"It is dangerous for you." Serenity broke free of Apollyon's grasp and stepped up to Lukas. "You are not strong enough. I have heard the stories from Apollyon. You are weak now. The Devil's voice is strong... he will speak to you. He will tempt you."

"I will not falter." Resolve filled Lukas's voice and his jaw set as he looked down at Serenity, his muscles bunching beneath his white shirt as he clenched his fists.

Annelie wished she could believe him.

Even Apollyon didn't look as though he fully believed that Lukas could resist any temptation that the Devil placed in his path. She wanted to tell him not to go, to remain with her instead, but forced herself to be silent. This was important to him. She had come here to support him, and she would do just that. She wouldn't shake his faith in her, and she would show her faith in him.

She would give him a reason to return to her, and the strength to face Hell and the Devil.

"I will make up a room. You can freshen up and perhaps we can go out together this evening and forget this dreary business." Apollyon looked at her. "We only have the one spare room. Will that prove a problem?"

Annelie felt Lukas's gaze on her too and met his eyes. If he was brave enough to go into Hell and risk himself to achieve his heart's desire, then she was brave enough to take the leap to have hers.

She smiled at Lukas.

"No problem at all."

CHAPTER 8

Lukas opened the bedroom door for Annelie. She smiled as she passed him and then stopped in the middle of the cream room, near the foot of the double bed that stood against the wall opposite him. It had been a nice evening, peaceful, and he felt as though he had made progress with Annelie. She had asked a lot of questions. Some of them he had answered, and others either Serenity or Apollyon had jumped on before he could find the right words.

It had gone well and Annelie seemed more comfortable around him now.

He wished he felt so relaxed.

He closed the door, swallowed his nerves, and turned to face her. She sat on the end of the bed, her hands pale against the dark brown covers.

"I can sleep on the floor." Lukas looked there, avoiding her gaze as his stomach twisted in knots and his heart began a slow, steady thumping against his ribs.

Would she make him take the floor or would she share the bed with him? He ached to sleep with her in his arms, to hold her close and savour the feel of her pressing against him, comforted by the knowledge she was safe and secure, protected from all the darkness in this world.

Darkness he would venture into come tomorrow.

Maybe his need to hold her while she slept was about more than just wanting to know she was safe. Maybe it was about giving him strength too, courage to face the darkness and a reason to survive it, to resist the temptations the Devil would throw at him the moment he entered his realm.

It had played on his mind at times throughout the evening, drawing him away from Annelie and the others. She noticed whenever his thoughts began to weigh on him, always touched his hand to bring him back to her, offering a soft smile when he looked at her that had helped him push away from fear of what might happen tomorrow and encouraging him to focus on the present instead, to make the most of this moment of calm with her.

"Apollyon and Serenity seem happy." Those softly spoken words had him coming back to her again, lifting his head and looking at her, wanting to see if she was pleased by that, if the discovery that an angel was in love with a witch and living with her gave her some relief, or comfort, and maybe even the strength to see that it was fine to be with him if she wanted it.

He nodded. "They are. I can feel it."

"You can?" Her fine eyebrows rose and she stood and then sat again.

"Is something wrong?" He sat beside her and she shuffled to face him, sitting at an angle with one leg on the bed.

"I don't know." She toyed with the hem of her dark t-shirt and shrugged. "I just feel a bit nervous."

Lukas chuckled low in his throat at that confession. "You are not the only one."

A brief smile tugged at her lips. It tugged at his heart too, had his smile faltering as a need to reassure her raced through him.

He took hold of her hands, clutched them in both of his and looked at them. They were small, delicate, so feminine. Her skin was a shade paler than his, soft where his had been roughened by centuries of fighting. He had done battle in countless wars, had faced legions of demonic angels and dangers that had cost him his life more than once, seeing him reborn in Heaven to start all over again, but this fight for her felt like the most dangerous, the most vital one to him.

If he didn't win this battle, he felt sure his life would be over. He wouldn't want to prove his innocence. He wouldn't want to serve Heaven again. He would head straight to Hell or worse.

"How can I convince you? I will do anything, Annelie." He toyed with her fingers, a strange tightness forming in his breast, one that had him desperate to find the answer because it might be his salvation.

She twisted her fingers around his, gently tangling them together. His heart beat hard against his chest as he waited for her to speak, balanced on the edge of falling and wild with a need to hear if there was anything that he could do to make her see that he loved her and that things between them could be heaven if she gave him a chance.

"You don't need to convince me. I'm not nervous about that." She stroked his hands and he looked up into her eyes. Her dark brown ones were full of honesty. She had looked at him so openly several times tonight and each had taken his breath away. Sometimes he had even fooled himself that he saw love in her eyes and that she was going to say that she wanted to be with him, and now it felt as though he was on the precipice of that happening. "I'm nervous about tomorrow."

"You will be safe here with Serenity." He clutched her hands tighter, a need to reassure her blasting through him together with a powerful desire to keep her safe.

He wouldn't let anything happen to her.

She shook her head. "No... not for me... for you, Lukas."

The sound of his name on her lips stirred his heart and he wrapped his fingers around hers, holding them tightly.

"I will be fine. I am stronger than Serenity thinks." He smiled at her, but it didn't alleviate the fear that shone in her eyes. "It is true that I am vulnerable to temptation, but I will not surrender to it. Nothing can take me away from you, Annelie. I will come back."

He wasn't sure what to do when she released his hands and threw her arms around his neck, burying her face against it. He flexed his fingers, hesitated for a heartbeat as the softness of her against him and the fact she was seeking comfort from him registered, and then wrapped his arms around her, holding her close.

She sighed into his throat, her warm breath teasing him, and he closed his eyes. It felt more than good to have her back in his arms. It was bliss. It was the first clear sign of her intent to give him the chance he so desperately wanted with her.

He smoothed his palm over her back, running it in circles he hoped would soothe her as she settled against him. She smelled so good, sweet and floral, and was so warm against him as she gripped his shirt, twisting the material into her fists. He leaned a little closer to her and breathed her in, and she lifted her head, bringing it up towards his. His stomach lightened as a new desire rose inside him, had his blood running hot despite the fear that flowed in his veins.

Would she reject him if he gave in to that desire?

He risked it and turned his head towards her and pressed a kiss to her red hair. She didn't push him away. He kissed her again and she murmured his name against his throat, nestled closer to him and twisted her head towards his.

"It has been a long day. You should get some sleep. I will take the floor." He stilled, waiting to hear what she would say.

She had to answer this time.

He needed to know where this was heading and whether she really was going to choose to be with him. It had been torture to be so close to her all day and not be able to act on his feelings for fear of scaring her away with them. He had wanted to hold her close so many times, to kiss her breathless and make sweet love to her. He had wanted everything they'd had in their night together.

Annelie emerged from his arms, her brown eyes dark as her pupils dilated to devour her irises, and stroked her fingertips over his chest, her touch light and maddening as fire swept over his skin in the wake of it.

"I don't want you to sleep on the floor." Her fingers brushed across his white shirt and down his arms, curling around his biceps.

"What do you want?" He held her gaze, needing to see it in her eyes when she said it so he would believe her and believe that this was happening.

Her shy smile stole his heart.

"I want you."

Lukas caught her around the waist, pulled her against him, and kissed her hard. She rewarded him sweetly, her lips dancing over his, stirring the passion that had lingered inside him since he had made love to her. He wanted to do that again, this time knowing that she was aware of what he was and everything was out in the open.

Her tongue swept across his lower lip and he touched it with his, encouraging her to let go of the restraint he could feel in her and embrace her passion as she had before. She moaned and stroked her tongue along the length of his, teasing him and luring him into deepening the kiss.

He didn't get the chance.

Surprise rippled through him as she shoved at his shoulders, pushing him back onto the bed, and he groaned as her body pressed against his, her breasts squashed against his arm and chest. She moaned and kissed him deeper. He craned his neck, hungry for more, and she broke away with a giggle as her teeth knocked his.

Lukas stared at the ceiling, breathing hard and silently begging her to come back to him. He wanted to kiss her again, needed to feel her body on his, and hungered to be inside her.

He pushed himself up on his elbows when she sat back, and groaned as she stripped her t-shirt off, revealing her bra-clad breasts. He reached for her, desperate with a need to cup her breasts and kiss them, but she evaded him, hopped from the bed, and tortured him by shimmying out of her jeans.

Too much.

He stretched for her again, willing her to come back to him so he could touch her, could caress and explore every sweet inch of her body. She smiled and shook her head, a wicked edge to her expression that had his heart beating harder, blood rushing faster.

He wanted to be angry with her for teasing him, but that emotion washed from him as she approached him and came to stand between his legs at the foot of the bed.

His pulse thrummed faster still, a dizzying beat that had his breaths coming in unsteady bursts as he waited.

Waited.

Annelie leaned over him and he swallowed hard as she fingered his belt and slowly undid it. He stared up at her face, watching the hunger growing in her eyes, resisting the temptation to move and join in, enjoying letting her be in control and being at her mercy because the look in her eyes promised it would be worth it.

She tugged on his belt to loosen it and made deft work of the buttons on his jeans. His cock throbbed when she brushed it through the thick material and he rolled his eyes, silently pleading her to touch him again.

She did.

She stroked her fingers over the hard outline of his shaft and then pushed her hands up, caressing his stomach. He closed his eyes when she mounted the bed to straddle his hips and unbuttoned his shirt. She moaned when she parted it and grazed her fingertips over his muscles.

He couldn't resist the temptation to watch her, wanting to see the passion in her eyes as she explored his body, needing to see if she liked it.

Her eyes were dark, filled with desire that echoed in him as she slowly traced the line of each muscle on his abdomen and then swept her hands over his chest. They settled there, her palms warm against him, and his heart beat harder.

The hunger in her eyes called to him, demanding he do something.

He bucked his hips against hers and she bit her lip and groaned. He did it again, eliciting another moan from her, and she dug her fingertips into his chest. Her eyelids slipped to half-mast when he ran his hands up her thighs. They were soft beneath his touch, warm and supple, the feel of them heightening his arousal and making his cock ache to be sheathed in her again.

He pushed his hands up, snagging the hem of her panties, and then continued, over the delicious curves of her waist and up to her breasts.

Her lips parted when he cupped them, thumbing her nipples through the thin material of her bra, and she sighed.

"Lukas."

It was heaven to hear her say his name with so much hunger and need. He ground his cock against her, rubbing her with it, and palmed her breasts. She leaned her head back and moaned, the breathy sound of it stirring him until he couldn't stop himself. He pulled her down to him and rolled her onto her back, nestling between her thighs.

Annelie claimed his lips, her mouth hot and hungry against his, devouring him and tempting him to unleash his own passion on her. He thrust against her again as he kissed her, teasing her with his tongue and his cock, and then broke away.

Her scowl faded as he made swift work of her bra and then sat back on his heels so he could remove her panties, slowing as he drew them down over her legs. She raised her feet and pressed them against his bare chest. His gaze lingered on the dark triangle of hair at the apex of her thighs. She had tasted so sweet. He wanted to taste her again.

Lukas pulled her underwear off over her feet, dropped them, and grasped her ankles. She smiled lazily up at him when he parted her legs and kissed her calf. He placed wet kisses along the length of her right leg, his eyes on his target, his hunger rising with each one.

When he reached the apex of her thighs, she spread her legs, an invitation that he wasn't going to turn down.

He kneeled on the edge of the bed.

Leaned over her.

Held her gaze as he lowered his head towards her hips.

CHAPTER 9

Lukas wanted to groan as he ran his tongue up through Annelie's plush petals, the sweetness of her hitting him hard, making him thirst for more.

She moaned and arched, the sound music to his ears, and he licked her again, flicking her pert bead this time. He rewarded each gasping moan with another swirl of his tongue around it and his cock ached when he slid his fingers down to her moist core. She shivered when he eased two fingers into her, burying them deep, and he shivered with her as she clenched her muscles around him.

Temptress.

He wanted to be inside her, thrusting deep and slow, drawing out their coupling this time and making her see just how good they could be together. He lapped at her, flicking his tongue over her sensitive nub, and pumped her with his fingers, rubbing the soft spot inside her until she moaned his name and begged for more. She tasted as divine as he remembered, sweet on his tongue and teasing his senses. He licked her harder, thrusting deeper with his fingers, picturing himself in her.

His cock throbbed at the images, pulsing against his underwear. It ached for relief, to feel her hands on it and her mouth.

Lukas groaned. Maybe next time. Right now, he wanted to be buried deep in her.

Annelie mewled when he drew his fingers out of her and stood. She frowned at him, her gaze dark with need, and then licked her lips when he pushed his jeans and boxer shorts down. She swayed her knees, enticing him, and he hurried, kicking his shoes off and stepping out of the rest of his clothes.

The moment he moved back to the bed, she parted her legs again, placing them either side of his. She reached up to him and he obeyed, covering her body with the length of his. The feel of her beneath him, her naked body against his, drove him close to the edge, and it was almost game over as he rubbed his cock through her folds, her heat scorching him.

He groaned and kissed her, fought to focus to keep his body under control. Her tongue tackled his, plundering his mouth, and she pushed him back to the edge when she rubbed herself against his hard length.

He thrust again, eager to be inside her, and then shifted backwards, breaking contact with her so he could claw back control. She gasped as he lowered his mouth to her breasts and tangled her fingers in his hair, holding him against her. He laved her nipple, circled it with the tip of his tongue, and then sucked it. She arched into him, pressing her breast into his mouth, and rocked her hips.

"Lukas."

The need she uttered his name with tore all restraint from him, shoved him over the edge.

He reached down to take hold of his cock. She was there before him, her warm hand wrapping around his hard length, and he stilled. Her eyes held his as she stroked him, running her thumb over the sensitive head to tease him. He moaned and closed his eyes, savouring the feel of her hands on him, gentle but firm, satiating his hunger for her.

Her other hand pressed against his chest and she pushed him up, coming with him and forcing him to kneel on the bed between her legs, his cock level with her face. She ran her fingers down the length of him and teased his balls, rolling them, sending a fierce hot shiver through him that had his legs trembling. He grunted when she wrapped her lips around his shaft and sucked it, stroking the blunt head with her tongue and gripping him with her other hand.

Lukas grasped her shoulders, squeezing them as she sucked him, taking more of him into her mouth and moving her hand in time with it. He thrust through the ring of her fingers and into her sweet mouth, groaning each time she swallowed him and with each roll of his balls.

He wanted more.

She moaned when he pumped into her, the sound of her pleasure sending a thrill through him. He struggled to keep his thrusts slow and shallow but it was difficult when it felt so good. Almost impossible as she tightened her grip on him and he had to bite his lip to stop himself from climaxing. He didn't want it to be over yet.

Annelie flicked her tongue over his crown and pumped him with her hand, pushing him to the very edge. Her breathy moans and the sounds of her sucking him were too much. He closed his eyes and thrust desperately into her mouth, breathing hard and moaning, clutching her shoulders. Her hand moved faster on him, mercifully swift and hard as she swallowed his cock in time with its movements.

His face twisted as he tried to hold off. Impossible. His eyes snapped open and he grunted her name as he filled her mouth with his seed. She moaned and continued to pump him, drawing out his climax and making him tremble as she swallowed and then lapped at the blunt crown.

Lukas remained kneeling on the bed between her legs when she released him and crashed back onto the mattress. Her rough breathing joined his, filling the room, and he stared at the far wall above the head of the bed, struggling to steady his heart, his legs trembling and weak.

He wanted her more than ever now but there was no chance of that happening yet.

He looked down at his softening cock and then at her. She blushed a deep shade of crimson and smiled shyly.

With a long sigh, he collapsed onto the bed beside her, still trying to catch his breath.

Annelie rolled onto her front and traced patterns on his bare chest, resting her chin on his shoulder. It tickled but he didn't stop her. He stared at her face, studying her beauty as her dark gaze followed her fingers across his body. Her cheeks were still red, matching the colour of her kiss-swollen lips and her hair.

He lazily reached over and stroked it, drained from his release and ready to fall asleep now. He couldn't though, not until he had made love to her.

He skimmed his hand over her shoulder and down her side. Her exploration of his body slowed when he neared her hips. She shifted back and he raised her leg, running his hand down the inside of her thigh towards her mound. Her eyes closed the moment he touched it, slipping his fingers back into her warm folds, and she sighed when he circled her aroused nub, teasing it, and then slid them downwards and into her core.

His cock twitched at the feel of her, desire reigniting as he pumped her slowly with his fingers, not wanting to make her climax, buying himself time to become aroused again.

Annelie rolled onto her back, her red hair fanned out across the bed, beautifully wanton and sensual. He gazed at her, thrusting his fingers into her warm depths, teasing her bead with his thumb whenever he had a chance. She raised her hips into his hand and moaned, tilting her head back at the same time.

She was stunning and he was beginning to feel that she was his.

He cast his gaze over her body, taking in the subtle curves and the delicious swell of her breasts.

She moaned again when he leaned over and sucked her right nipple into his mouth. His fingers delved deeper into her and his cock stirred, growing hard at the slippery feel of her and the sound of her sweet quiet groans.

"Lukas," she whispered and he released her breast and looked at her.

She stared deep into his eyes, hers full of fire and passion, hunger that he wanted to satisfy. Her eyes slipped shut for a moment and then she opened them again, meeting his once more, looking so deep into them that he felt as though she was looking straight down into his heart.

What was she trying to see?

Did she want to see if he loved her?

He did.

He ran a hand over her hair and stroked her cheek, holding her gaze as he opened his heart to her.

He loved her and needed her more than anything.

She gasped when he plunged his fingers into her again and smiled at him, the passion in her eyes turning to warmth. Had she seen the answer she wanted?

He would say the words if she needed to hear them and he was sure that they wouldn't make her run away.

She jerked her chin up and he obeyed. He pressed against her side and kissed her, pouring his love for her into it so she would feel what this meant to him, and what *she* meant to him. She moaned and he felt her smile against his mouth when he thrust his hard cock against her hip.

"Make love to me," she whispered into his mouth.

He would. He would show her without words what he felt for her and when she was ready to hear them, he would put those feelings into three words that he meant with all of his heart.

Lukas moved between her hips, took hold of his cock, and guided himself into her. She sighed when he eased into her, fusing their bodies as one, and he groaned with her when he was as deep as she could take him. He stayed there a moment, absorbing the feel of her. He never wanted to leave.

He leaned on his elbows, claimed her lips and kissed her softly as he thrust slowly into her, long strokes that had her moaning each time he withdrew. He kept the pace unhurried, kissing her and running his hands through her hair, wanting this to be about more than just sex.

This was how it should have been last night.

It should have been more than it had been. It should have been about passion and their feelings, a slow coupling, a moment of bliss for both of them.

It should have been making love.

Annelie buried her fingers into his hair, tangled the lengths around them and then skimmed her hands down to his shoulders as her lips played softly with his. She ran her feet over his legs, raised her hips and moaned in time with him as he slid deeper. He breathed slowly, his heart beating in a fast symphony with hers, lost in the feel of her.

Sheer bliss.

She moaned against his lips and deepened the kiss, and he sensed the need rising inside her, felt the wildness of it in her kiss as she seized command of it, bending him to her will. He held her hip and drove into her, gently quickening the pace of his thrusts to give her what she needed. She tensed around him and gripped his shoulders, pressing her fingers into his muscles. He kept going, swallowing her moans, hungrily devouring each one that he elicited.

"More," she whispered against his lips and he obliged, tensing and pumping her faster, keeping his strokes long.

He wanted more too. He wanted it harder and rougher, but this wasn't about that sort of lovemaking. This was more than that. This was about feelings, and being one, and her acceptance of him.

Her kisses turned hot and fierce and her body clenched his again, luring him into surrendering to the need that blazed through him. He found the strength to resist it and keep his pace steady, slowly driving her towards her climax and allowing it to build so it would be bliss when it happened.

She moaned and held him to her, tilted her head away from his as her brow furrowed and her lips parted. He groaned and buried his face in her throat, concentrated on how it felt to be with her and her feelings as he pushed them both higher. They were warm, suffusing every inch of his body along with his own emotions. They were as he had suspected and he smiled at the feel of them, knowing that she loved him too and that it was why she had given him a second chance. She moaned each time their bodies met, soft and gasping, and he kissed her throat.

"Lukas," she whispered and he murmured against her neck when he felt fear surfacing in her feelings.

He was there with her. She didn't need to be afraid. They were both falling.

No.

They had both fallen.

And she had been the one to catch him and give him a reason to go on.

And he loved her so much for that.

Annelie gasped, tensed and shook in his arms as her body quivered around his, the feel of her climaxing pushing him right to the edge. He grunted and thrust deeper, harder, curling his hips and unable to hold back now he was on the precipice.

She kissed him again and clenched her trembling body around his.

Too much.

He jerked to a halt inside her, his breath leaving him in a rush as his cock throbbed hard, pulsing and spilling inside her, and heat ricocheted through him, had every muscle shaking as stars winked across his vision. She moaned and rolled her hips, tearing a groan from him as she throbbed around his length.

When his body finally stopped trembling and he could move again, he kissed her, head foggy and every inch of him hazy as he brushed his lips across hers. She lazily kissed him back, twined her fingers in his hair and stroked her tongue along the seam of his lips. He groaned and rolled with her, so she was on top of him.

She sighed, rested her elbows above his shoulders on the bed, and wrapped her hands over the top of his head as she kissed him.

She didn't have to worry about him going to Hell. He was stronger than she thought, and he had her to thank for that. She gave him the strength to go with Apollyon and face temptation in order to find a way of clearing his name. It wasn't just that she had told him not to give up, or that she had come with him to Paris. It was because she loved him that he could do it.

Lukas stroked her sides and she giggled, wriggling on him. He smiled at the sound of it and how relaxed things were between them again.

It was because he loved her that he could do it.

Annelie drew back and looked down at him, her smile beautiful and her eyes full of the love she wouldn't admit.

He wasn't just doing this to clear his name. He was doing it so he could be the man he used to be again, and not the one he had become because of his punishment. He wanted to be strong again so she would love him even more and would never leave him. He wanted to be with her always.

This was more than a desire to return to his old life.

It was a desire to make a new one with her, and he would do whatever he had to in order to make that happen.

Stroking the rogue strands of her red hair from her face, he stared deep into her eyes.

She had made her decision.

She had chosen to be with him.

Now he had a decision of his own to make.

She wouldn't understand it at first, but in part it was a decision that she had to make too. He still wasn't sure what he was going to do, but his heart said to be with her whichever way she wanted.

He tucked her hair behind her ear and grazed his thumb across her cheek.

He would let her decide.

When he had found a way to free himself of his punishment and had restored his name, he would ask her what she wanted and he would abide by her decision.

Even if it meant he never flew again.

CHAPTER 10

Annelie dried herself off, warm from her shower and relaxed even when she knew what lay ahead of her.

She leaned back and glanced through the open bathroom door at Lukas where he lounged on the double bed wearing only his underwear.

Temptation personified.

He couldn't have looked more relaxed as he noticed her watching him and his green gaze came to rest on her. His eyes darkened as he studied her, banked heat flaring in them again. If he kept looking at her like that, with so much passion in his eyes, she was going to demand an encore to last night.

She smiled mischievously as she dropped her towel and his gaze instantly fell to her bare body. His lips parted and he sat up on the end of the bed, desire mounting in his eyes as he held his hand out to her.

She took a deep breath to find her courage and walked into the room, swaying her hips just enough that his attention snapped there. The hunger that flooded his handsome face gave her the strength she was looking for. Last night had been wonderful, long lazy spells of making love and connecting to each other in the most intimate way. She wanted to feel that again.

His eyes roamed over her body, gradually working their way up, and were on her face when she stopped in front of him, so close to him he had to tip his head back to look into her eyes.

Annelie stepped between his knees at the foot of the bed and swept her fingers through the messy tangle of his fair hair, holding his gaze the whole time. His pupils dilated as she stroked the strong line of his jaw, the stubble there scratching her fingertips. She tilted his head back and kissed him, long and slow. Her body heated, blood on fire as his lips swept across hers, fanning the flames until they blazed like an inferno inside her and she needed more from him.

He groaned as she broke away from his lips.

She glanced down, an ache settling in her belly that demanded she sate it, and moaned as she raked her eyes over him and found he was hard, tenting the black material of his boxers.

He hissed in his breath when she ran her fingers over the outline of his cock and closed his eyes. The sense of empowerment that rushed through her, born of how he reacted to her, was dizzying, drugging, and she couldn't stop herself from pushing his shoulder, forcing him to lay back on the bed. He went willingly, gaze scalding her as she climbed astride him. His hands settled on her knees and she licked her lips when he ran them up her thighs, his touch so light that it tickled and a shiver danced through her.

She rocked on him as she explored his body with her fingers, trying to decide what to do with him. The look in his eyes, on his face, said that he was at her mercy. He would do whatever she wanted. Perhaps it was time they turned up the heat a little and she lived out another of the dreams she'd had of them together.

He moaned when she dismounted and his eyes rolled closed as she stripped off his underwear. The sight of him gloriously naked before her sent a pulse through her and she clenched her muscles to make the most of the feeling, aroused by the thought of what she was going to do.

Kneeling on the bed beside him, she waited for him to open his eyes and then moved so she was astride his face, looking down at his hard length. She had never done this before but she had dreamed about it several times, and each time it had been delicious.

Lukas groaned, grabbed her hips, and guided her down to his mouth. He licked her and she shivered again, moaning quietly as her gaze fell on his shaft and she ran her hand down it, exposing the sensitive crown. He moaned with her when she took him into her mouth, sucking him and swirling her tongue around the blunt head as he licked and flicked her. It was as good as she had dreamed it would be and she couldn't get enough of worshipping his body as he pleasured hers.

His grip on her tightened and she moaned against his cock each time he licked the length of her, gasped and sucked him harder, wrapping her fingers around the length of his shaft, when he plunged a finger into her and pumped slowly. She wanted more, but she didn't want to climax yet. She wanted to push Lukas to the edge and keep him there, until he felt as hungry as she was.

She slowed her sucking and released him, teasing him with her tongue instead. He groaned into her, suckling her bead, and thrust through the ring of her fingers. That groan became a moan of frustration when she pulled away from him. It was too much. She wanted him inside her, not his finger.

Annelie rolled off him and he pulled her to him and covered her with his body, kissing her and stealing her breath away. She wrapped her arms around him, matching his passion and hunger, rubbing herself against his hard length. She wanted that inside her now, satisfying her need, scratching her itch. She needed to be one with him, lost in him for a moment, so she didn't think about what was going to happen tonight and so she was sure he would come back to her.

She needed him to come back to her.

She loved him too much to lose him.

Lukas grabbed her hip and thrust the length of his cock against her, teasing her and bringing her close to the edge again. She kissed him harder, driving him on, tackling his tongue with hers and wishing he was inside her.

She pushed him onto his back again and moaned as she rubbed herself against his shaft.

"Lukas." The breathy sound of her voice startled her and she pushed herself into saying what she wanted. "Take me."

He sat up, kissed her and palmed her breasts with one hand, the other settling in the arch of her back. He slid it down to cup her backside and kneaded it.

"Take me," she whispered against his lips and he lifted her and placed her down on the bed.

He covered her, spreading her legs, and took hold of his hard cock. She moaned when he eased the full length of it into her, pressed his hands against the bed at her sides and loomed over her. She took hold of his biceps, her eyes darting up to meet his.

Their green depths were dark with desire. Need that echoed inside her.

His muscles tensed, taut beneath her fingers, speaking of his strength. It thrilled her and part of her wanted him to use that strength on her, ached to beg him to reveal it to her so she could revel in it. He leaned down, settling on his elbows, and wrapped his hands over her shoulders, gripping them tightly. The delicious feel of him withdrawing almost all of the way before plunging back into her ripped a moan from her throat.

Annelie closed her eyes and focused on where their bodies met as he thrust hard and deep into her, a wildness about him that had her arousal soaring higher, need twisting tighter inside her. His grip on her shoulders tightened, fingertips digging in, and he moaned into her ear with each deep plunge of his cock. She lifted her hips off the bed and groaned with him, encouraging him to let go and take her.

It was bliss to feel him so rough and commanding, pleasuring her with his passion and hunger.

"More," she breathed.

He grunted, kissed and nipped at her throat and thrust harder into her, his pace quickening until she couldn't take any more. She reached above her for the pillows and clenched them tight in her fingers, as he drove deep into her and groaned, trembling as his cock kicked and throbbed.

Annelie moaned as he pulsed inside her, sending ripples of pleasure through her that had her straining for her own release. He slid a hand down between her legs and rubbed her bead, his fingers flicking over it, and she jerked against him and cried out as hazy warmth spread through her and her breath caught in her throat.

Lukas lazily peppered her neck with kisses, one hand holding her hip, as though he didn't want to leave her body yet. She lay beneath him, feeling his heart hammering against her chest, out of time with her own, and his warm breath skittering over her skin.

"Annelie," he whispered and she murmured, not quite able to speak yet. "I... I will come back."

She looked up at him as he drew back, awareness of what he had really wanted to say rolling through her.

She closed her eyes when he pulled out of her and sighed when he collapsed onto the bed beside her and tugged her over to lie against him. His body moulded against hers, his front to her back, and he kissed her shoulder, pressing his lips there.

Unease rippled through her, fear rising again, and not just of saying what she felt in her heart. She was afraid that he wasn't strong enough, even when she knew deep inside that he was, and that he wouldn't come back to her. She kept telling herself that he would come back, that he was strong and would survive whatever Hell threw at him, but her heart wasn't listening. It was a timid thing in her chest, beating wildly as thoughts of him in Hell tore at her, ripped at her own strength and bred doubt.

She couldn't lose him.

Annelie rolled to face him, needing to look into his eyes and know his feelings for her, and needing him to see hers. His lips curved into a slight smile, one that had an edge of fear to it. It wasn't fear of the Devil. It was fear of what was happening between them and something else that she couldn't quite put her finger on.

She stroked his cheek, holding his green gaze, and smiled for him. His breathing settled, slowing along with hers, and he pulled her closer, his hand warm against her back.

She swallowed her heart and swept the hair from his forehead.

He was so handsome, a man beyond her dreams.

Her fallen angel.

She looked deep into his eyes, seeing all his feelings there. The ones he had been afraid to tell her. So much affection and tenderness. So much love. It was strange to have a man who had always looked so strong before look so vulnerable. It made her realise the power she had over him and how much she meant to him.

How afraid he was of losing her too.

She skimmed her hand down to his jaw and cupped his cheek.

"Lukas," she murmured and some of the fear in his eyes drifted away, his irises brightening as the dark shadows lifted from his heart.

Did he know what she wanted to say?

Was it the same as what he had wanted to say but then failed to voice?

She swept her thumb across his cheek.

One of them had to take the leap, and it had to be her.

He would say it if she gave him time, but he needed to hear it more than she did. He needed it in order to give him the strength to go to Hell and come back again.

She whispered, "I love you."

The smile that graced his lips quickly became a grin and he pulled her flush against him and kissed the breath out of her, filling her with lightness and warmth that chased away all her fears and her doubts, because it was out there now. She had taken the leap, and now all he had to do was catch her.

"I love you too," Lukas murmured between kisses, soft and tender, his voice full of the feelings behind those words, and she knew he meant them from the bottom of his heart.

Now she wasn't afraid.

Now she knew he would return to her.

CHAPTER 11

Lukas was grinning when Apollyon started their descent into Hell. It wasn't just the fact that he was flying by proxy. It was the fact that Annelie loved him and had managed to say the words. He silently thanked her all over again for finding the courage to tell him, to give him the added strength and resolve to return to her and resist the temptation the Devil would offer.

"You are heavier than you look," Apollyon muttered darkly from behind him, holding him under his arms, his black and gold armour hard against Lukas's back. "But I commend you on your desire to abide by the rules of your punishment."

"Do not think me a saint." Lukas lifted his feet to avoid a rock that jutted out and stared at the glowing orange line beneath him. Black jagged walls blurred past them and Apollyon beat his wings to slow their descent. Lukas's shoulders ached, his wings wanting out, but he denied them and focused below him. "I have broken rules of our kind."

"Really?" Apollyon sounded curious now. "Do tell."

The fiery line grew brighter and thicker.

"I have tasted alcohol." He jerked forwards when Apollyon suddenly halted in the air.

Lukas could sense his desire to turn him and look into his eyes.

Instead of doing so, Apollyon swooped down so fast that Lukas's stomach turned, and landed them hard on the black broken ground of Hell.

Apollyon released him and Lukas stumbled towards the edge of the cragged plateau they were on and barely stopped himself from falling over it.

Flames licked up the sides of a crevasse in front of him and he didn't dare look down. The bottomless pit was not something an angel should look into. Hearing the demons and feeling them was bad enough. He didn't need to see them, not when he was so susceptible to their whispers.

"You have tasted alcohol?" The surprise in Apollyon's voice matched that on his face when Lukas turned his back to the bottomless pit.

Lukas changed his appearance, removing his usual attire and replacing it with his gold-edged white armour.

It had been too long since he had looked his normal self and not like a mortal. He hadn't been allowed to wear his armour in Heaven when he had gone there to lodge an appeal, had had the ability to call it to his body taken from him the moment he had decided to head to the white fortress. Because they had feared he might also call his weapons and dare to attack a realm he loyally served?

He would never do such a thing.

He looked down at his armour, finding the strength that had started to bleed from him in it. No angel would admit it, but their armour was important to them, a symbol of what they were and their allegiance. It was more than that too, it was a possession that had been theirs from birth, something that had always been with them, protected them from harm and gave them the power to fight for what they believed in.

He had denied himself the sight of his armour for the last three years, had been too ashamed to look at it, but now it felt like a symbol of strength to him again. It felt like a part of him again. Annelie had restored his belief in himself, had shown faith in him that had given him the courage to wear his armour again, and to wear it proudly. This was who he was, no matter what Heaven believed. He was still the angel he had once been.

No, he was more than that male now, made stronger by Annelie's love.

The fierce golden light from the rivers of lava that surrounded the plateau reflected off the gold detailing on his greaves, breastplate, vambraces and the slats that protected his hips, making them shine.

It felt good to wear his armour again.

Not only because it made him feel powerful, home again in a way.

But also because it was far cooler in Hell without restrictive human clothing covering every inch of his body.

His white wings unfurled and he spread them, extending them to their full span, and sighed at the feel of having them free again at last.

Apollyon gave him a look that said he was waiting, his blue eyes still filled with curiosity, and it took Lukas a moment to remember what they had been discussing before he had been swept up in the way it felt to wear his armour again.

"I do not recommend alcohol." Lukas rolled his shoulders and flapped his wings, not enough to lift him off the ground, but enough to bring his ruffled feathers into place and give him a glimpse of how exhilarating it would be to fly again.

He had missed it these past few days. Never before had he realised just how much flying meant to him.

Could he really sacrifice such a thing if Annelie asked it of him?

"What happened?" Apollyon held his hand out, pointing towards an area away from the fiery furnace of the pit.

There was nothing around them but rough black shards of rock and blistering flames.

And a fortress of towering obsidian spires in the distance to his left, but he kept his eyes firmly away from that.

"I got drunk." Lukas followed him across the uneven charred ground, coughing as he tried to breathe normally. The air choked his lungs, rich with sulphur and acrid. He wasn't sure how Apollyon had stood being assigned to this realm for centuries. It would have killed him. "I got drunk, I made love with Annelie and then I had a terrible headache and a dry mouth when I awoke the next day."

"You made love when drunk?" Apollyon stopped and frowned over his shoulder at him.

Lukas smiled sheepishly. "It seems alcohol works on us as it does on humans. I had no inhibitions. All of my reservations disappeared and I surrendered to temptation and did as I pleased. I kissed her and then things just happened. I felt brave and invincible."

"And then you had a headache." Apollyon's frown deepened.

He didn't really want to remember that part. "For a day... it was not pleasant."

"But you were not punished. Even though you are banished, they would have still punished you if you had broken a rule." Apollyon started walking again, his face twisting into a thoughtful expression as he stared at the rocks jutting up ahead of him. "So we can drink alcohol without castigation."

"It would appear so."

His friend smiled. "Interesting."

Lukas smiled too. He didn't need to ask to know what Apollyon was thinking. His fellow angel would soon be experimenting with alcohol. No angel could resist trying something new, especially when it had previously been forbidden.

They moved further from the pit and the heat abated a little, but the sharp acid tang still filled the air and stole his breath. Lukas no longer envied Apollyon for his position as the guardian of this place.

Heaven always spoke of it as an important position, one that all angels should hope to achieve, one sacred and richly rewarding.

Apollyon's sour expression as he cast his blue gaze over their grim surroundings made Lukas think it was quite the opposite. Apollyon looked positively displeased at having to return and kept casting his gaze upwards, towards the dark ceiling above them. It had closed the moment they were through, sealing them in Hell, and Lukas missed the sight of the sky already.

Had Apollyon felt that way too for all the years he had guarded the pit?

A young angel dressed in black armour similar to Apollyon's stood and walked towards them. His face lit up when he saw Apollyon and Lukas hid his smile when Apollyon sighed. Clearly, he didn't enjoy the adoration that his title of 'Defeater of the Devil' garnered him either.

Apollyon waved the dark-haired angel away before he could speak. He dutifully nodded and went elsewhere, leaving them alone.

"A temp. All they could offer was some halfwit youngling to replace me in a temporary fashion. I will still have to return in four hundred and thirty two years and seventy six days to send the Devil back to the bottomless pit at this rate." Apollyon scowled in the direction of the fortress that loomed in the centre of the pit when a dark voice curled up from it and around them, words that conveyed both the challenge issued and the hatred borne by its owner.

The Devil.

Lukas attempted to shut the voice out, afraid that he would succumb to it and that the Devil would discover he was fallen.

It slithered around him, a treacherous snake that felt as though it was for his ears only. Lukas tried not to listen but it was impossible to resist the lure as it whispered and hissed, offering up sweet words like honey to his ears and his heart.

He could have vengeance.

No. Such an offer wouldn't tempt him. The Devil would make good on his word but it wouldn't satisfy Lukas. He wanted to prove his innocence, not seek out retribution.

He could have Annelie.

Forever.

Lukas stopped, closed his eyes and clenched his fists, battling the temptation those words represented.

He wanted that more than anything. He wanted Annelie to be his and to be with him forever.

No.

He didn't need the Devil's help in order to have that. He could have it and he was willing to sacrifice something to achieve it. Annelie was up there waiting for him to return. He couldn't disappoint her by being so weak and listening to the Devil. He was strong because of her and he would no longer hear the Devil's seductive words.

He wouldn't surrender to temptation.

"Ignore him." Apollyon took hold of Lukas's arm and led him around the rocks. "He will get bored soon enough and leave you alone."

Lukas hoped that was true as the Devil's words ran in his head on repeat, offering forever with Annelie over and over again. A true forever. He clenched his jaw and fought to ignore the wretch, because that sort of forever would come at a high price, if the Devil could even deliver on it. He wasn't sure the creature had that much power.

A dark snarl tore through his mind.

Apollyon's grip on him tightened and his strength seemed to seep into Lukas, giving a boost to his own that allowed him to push back against the Devil as Apollyon growled dark words in the direction of the fortress.

When Lukas looked at Apollyon, his eyes were glowing blue, sharp and focused beyond him.

His friend glanced at him and shook his head, as if trying to shake off whatever darkness had come over him. It lingered though, and something told Lukas his anger hadn't been born of the Devil trying to tempt him. It had been born of something else.

"What's wrong?" He went to look over his shoulder towards the fortress.

Apollyon stopped him with three words.

"Rook isn't dead."

"What?" Lukas snapped back to his friend, unable to believe what he was hearing.

"He wasn't reborn. Not in Heaven anyway. I didn't want to tell you all until I knew more, because there are still some things I don't understand... I wanted to be able to tell you good news, but I am not sure there will be any good news to give." Apollyon released him and paced a short distance away, frustration rolling off him as he heaved a long sigh and looked into the darkness beyond the shimmering silvery pool. His shoulders lifted in another sigh and something akin to sorrow crossed his tight features. "I saw Rook here."

"Impossible." Because they had searched for him all those centuries ago and hadn't found a trace of him or Isadora. "Unless..."

"Unless he was hidden from us. Even freshly fallen into the Devil's service, I still would have been able to sense him. We had a bond, one the

Devil must have known about. He must have hidden Rook from us, concealing him in the fortress."

Because the layers of darkness that surrounded it were too thick for any angel to penetrate.

Rook was alive and in the service of the Devil?

He was only just coming to terms with that when Apollyon rocked his world on its axis again.

"Isadora is alive too."

"Is she here?" Lukas cast a glance over the forbidding black landscape that stretched into shadows around him.

Was that the reason Rook had chosen to serve Hell instead? Had he been swayed by the Devil, made to believe that he could continue to protect Isadora if he succumbed to temptation and pledged allegiance to him?

"No," Apollyon said in a grim tone. "I saw her in Paris. She was being... taken, I think. There's a group abducting witches... Lukas... she's alive... somehow..."

He knew what Apollyon meant by that. No witch could live that long through natural means. They had lifespans that extended beyond a normal human's, but not by centuries, and she had to be thousands of years old by now.

"You are sure it was her?" He shrugged when Apollyon shot him a look that said he was definitely sure and he didn't like Lukas questioning his ability to recognise her. "I was just checking."

Because it all seemed so impossible.

"Does Rook know she's alive?" Lukas ignored the dark voice that cut through the thick choking air to seep into his mind, warning him to leave Hell.

The Devil didn't like what they were discussing. The smile that tugged at the corners of Apollyon's lips said he had received the same message and it pleased him. Had Apollyon chosen to tell Lukas about Rook and Isadora here, where the Devil could hear them, in order to draw the wretch out?

To test him?

"I have the feeling if Rook knew she was alive, in danger, that he would do something about it," Apollyon drawled, his smile stretching as the Devil snarled at them to leave, detailed the ways he was going to rip them apart if they didn't, how he was going to destroy them and send them back to Heaven in pieces.

Apollyon grinned.

"Someone is tetchy today." He spread his black wings and beat them. "Perhaps I should do a lap of Hell and see if I can find Rook."

Lukas covered his ears as a whisper roared in his mind.

Annelie could be his forever... if he took Apollyon down. No strings attached. No lies. Destroy the dark angel, and claim her as his prize.

He swayed as his knees weakened, the voice seeping from his mind into his limbs, poisoning him and birthing a terrifying need, a desire that had him rocking forwards, towards Apollyon.

Because he wanted Annelie to be his forever.

His hands twitched at his sides.

Power accumulated there as his spear began to form.

He could have that forever.

He just had to take Apollyon down.

CHAPTER 12

Apollyon's blue gaze darted to Lukas's hands and he lunged towards him and gripped Lukas's wrists before he could finish calling his weapon to him. Lukas growled and tried to twist free.

"Do not listen to him," Apollyon said to him and then raised his voice, bellowing, "Leave him alone. You want to fight, you can fight me yourself."

The grip on his wrists tightened as he fought to free himself.

Words swam in his hazy mind.

"Look at me, Lukas."

He struggled to focus, Apollyon swimming in his vision, blurring with the darkness.

"Annelie is waiting for you. She wouldn't want you to do this. Fight him."

It was easier said than done. He focused on Annelie, on the fact she was waiting for him in Paris and he had promised to return to her, and also the fact he didn't want to hurt his friend. He focused on her love for him, and the love he had for her, and the bond he shared with Apollyon, using it to push out the dark tendrils wrapping around his heart.

The Devil's voice faded from a roar to a whisper and he kept on pushing, his entire body trembling, every muscle shaking as he began to weaken, resisting the Devil taking its toll on him and stripping him of his strength.

The hold the Devil had on him suddenly disappeared and he slumped forwards, would have hit the black basalt if Apollyon hadn't caught him.

"I am sorry," Apollyon murmured and held him up as he struggled to catch his breath and waited for his strength to return. "I should have thought about what would happen before provoking him."

"But at least we know he values Rook now." Lukas gripped Apollyon's shoulders and hauled himself back onto his feet.

Which wasn't good news.

Getting to Rook was going to prove difficult, if not impossible. The Devil would throw his legions at them if they tried, would seek to take them down. He had slain entire squadrons of angels of Heaven in the past in order to protect only a few demonic angels he favoured, pulling out all the stops to ensure they remained his.

Apollyon didn't look deterred by that. "I will find a way to reach him. I do not need to sway him back to our side. I do not even need him to remember who he was or who I am. I only need him to remember her."

"Why?" Lukas released Apollyon and straightened, his knees no longer shaking beneath him.

Apollyon looked out across the black lands. "Because he was in love with her."

It was news to Lukas. He had noticed Rook had been protective of Isadora, but had put it down to his duty as her guardian angel. But then, he had never known love himself back then. It was possible that Rook had been in love with her. He had certainly been crazed when she had been taken from him, had flown into Hell without a second's pause to reach her and save her from the Devil, only to never return.

Lukas would do the same for Annelie. He would do whatever it took to keep her safe from harm, to protect her. He would fight the Devil himself if he had to.

The Devil snickered at that.

Lukas let it slide, because he was well aware that his strength was nothing compared with the Devil's and he wouldn't stand a chance if he fought him. It wouldn't stop him though.

Apollyon took hold of his arm, leading him towards the pool. "We will talk more about this later, away from here. Come, we should make haste. I think we have lingered here long enough."

Lukas couldn't have agreed more.

He wanted to be back in the mortal world, where the air was fresh and clean.

He wanted to see Annelie again.

The light from the pool was bright, catching on the intricate gold metalwork on Apollyon's black armour and casting a golden glow over his exposed skin. Lukas stepped up beside him as he stopped at the edge of the pool and looked down into it. He had never seen such a thing. Images flickered past him, so fast that he could barely keep up. They swirled and changed, and his head spun with them.

"It takes time to get used to." Apollyon crouched next to the pool and Lukas followed suit. "Touch it and you will see what your heart desires."

Lukas hesitated and then reached a hand out and gently dipped his finger into the pool. It was cold. The liquid on his finger when he withdrew it was black, not bright like the water in front of him, and he shook it away, not liking the feel of it on his skin.

The pool shimmered and the image changed.

He leaned forwards, eager to see what it could show him, and his eyebrows rose when the scene took shape and it was familiar.

Apollyon grinned.

In front of them, Annelie and Serenity were sitting on the roof terrace surrounded by candles, sharing a bottle of wine under a dimly starlit night. Lukas's heart beat harder, pounding at the sight of Annelie wearing one of Serenity's small dresses. It was pale, flecked with shapes he couldn't make out, and fitted snugly to her frame, emphasising everything that made him ache for her.

"Is everything alright between you now?" Apollyon's voice cut into his thoughts of Annelie and Lukas looked across at him. He nodded. Apollyon's blue gaze returned to the pool and his eyebrows knitted. "What will you do? She's human... will you forsake your wings and choose a mortal life for her? It is not an easy path to take. They do not let you go so easily. I speak from experience. It took long months to argue my contract with Heaven and even now, I am not wholly free to do as I please. It is only my contract with Serenity which keeps me on Earth."

Lukas's gaze dropped to the pool and Annelie. Apollyon was lucky in that regard. He had spoken to him about it last night and it was Serenity's magic that had allowed her to call to him and contract with him. Annelie didn't have a voice to call him with.

"I am still not sure. It is a decision I wish to make with her, when I am certain that it will not be one I will regret." Or one she would regret.

Apollyon's gaze landed on him again. "You fear she will leave you still?"

Lukas stared at her. Did he? Was that why he hesitated whenever he thought about sacrificing his immortality for her? It was a lot to give up and if she changed her mind about him, he wouldn't be able to take it back. It would be gone forever. He would be mortal and alone.

Annelie laughed about something and he wished he could hear her and know what she and Serenity were talking about but they were speaking too quietly. They were both smiling and it felt wrong to spy on her, even when he was an angel and he was drawn to watching.

She had said that she loved him, and he knew it was the truth.

If he surrendered his wings, would she remain with him?

"There is another way." Apollyon's deep voice cut into his thoughts.

Lukas's eyes darted to him.

"It is dangerous to ask her to go through such a thing, and it is still a decision that we will need to make in time rather than now." He held Apollyon's gaze and he nodded, the look in his dark eyes saying that he was aware that asking a mortal to walk the path to immortality and face the trials was as bad as asking an angel to sacrifice his immortality and wings.

The Devil laughed.

Black words rolled up from the pit in a belch of flames and filled the air around Lukas and Apollyon. This time it was a promise to both of them.

Immortality for their loves.

Apollyon cast a glare at the pit and spat out a curse so dark that the ground trembled. The Devil laughed again. Lukas shunned his voice and his promise, finding it easier when he was looking at Annelie.

In time, he would speak to Annelie about such things, but not yet. It was too soon to be discussing whether to seek immortality for her or surrender his own.

One day.

He would wait until she mentioned it and then he would know she was serious about him.

"Focus." Apollyon waved his hand over the pool and a rush of images replaced that of Annelie and Serenity. "Women are a distraction."

Lukas couldn't agree more.

He pushed Annelie from his mind, fixed his thoughts on the night he had witnessed the explosion, and touched the pool again.

The images distorted and a new one surfaced.

It was the old brick factory building.

The dark area outside it was quiet, not a vehicle or person in sight. He leaned over, his gaze darting about to take everything in. Someone moved inside the building and then a black van pulled up outside.

Two men came out.

Apollyon snarled, "Demons."

Lukas stared at the men, studying them. Apollyon was right. They were demons in the guise of young men. They walked around the back of the van and opened the doors. He frowned when they started taking black sacks out of the vehicle and carrying them into the building.

A second van pulled up and another man got out. Demon. Three demons and what looked like bodies.

"The people you apparently killed were already dead." Apollyon's voice was dark as midnight and Lukas could feel his unease.

It rippled through him, echoing his own feelings.

"But why?" He frowned at the pool.

It didn't make sense that only demons were involved.

They had to have known someone on his side of the fight, someone who could have set him up and who could have stopped Heaven from seeing them. The demons hadn't been there in any of the records he had seen. There had been no one in them. Not even the vehicles. Only an angel's power could have shielded them from Heaven's watchers.

That angel would have to be powerful.

And Lukas had a feeling he knew who it was.

There was only one angel in this whole affair who Lukas had ever thought capable of being involved, and it was the one he had accused at his appeal.

The door of the factory opened and that angel walked out, his white wings furled tightly against his back and his white armour matching Lukas's.

His commander.

Amaer.

The older man motioned to the three demons and they hurried forwards, ferrying the bodies into the building and returning with empty black sacks. Lukas watched them, trying to figure out what had happened that night and why his commander had been involved.

It slowly dawned on him.

"A month before this night, I saw my commander with a group of men. They were different to these ones but some demons can shift skin. I was curious as to why my commander was meeting mortals without changing his appearance and hiding his wings but did not hear what was being said." Lukas cursed himself for his own stupidity. "I later asked my commander what he had been doing."

"Was anyone else present at the time?" Apollyon glared at the images in the pool.

Lukas shook his head. "He denied meeting anyone and said that I had been overworked recently and perhaps needed time to rest. I refused his offer and said I had not imagined seeing him. He had not been in mortal guise. He insisted that it was not him, and then parted ways with me. Things went back to normal after that and I thought nothing more of it."

"He had hoped to silence you by pinning this crime on you, and he had done a good job of it until now. Whatever he was doing, it involved the death of those mortals." Apollyon frowned. "They were covering their trail for some reason."

"We need to find out what it was." Lukas stood when an image of him appeared in the pool, landing gracefully in the empty parking lot of the building.

A second later, the factory exploded, hurling him through the air.

Apollyon caught his wrist and Lukas looked at him.

"It is not our area." Apollyon stood and cast his hand over the pool. The image rewound to the point where his commander had been visible with the demons. "I will take the evidence to the authorities and you will wait with the females for my return. Heaven's Court will assign a specialist to assess the evidence and to deal with your commander and discover what these demons were doing."

"I will go too." Because he needed to be there, needed to hear them say they had been wrong and had to be sure they were going to do something.

"No." Apollyon looked thoughtfully at the pool and then into his eyes. "You have been through enough and it will be better if they heard this from me... take care of Annelie and Serenity. I do not want them to be alone."

Lukas frowned at that.

Was Apollyon insinuating that his commander might dare attack the women when Apollyon announced his evidence to the court?

It would be easy for his commander to discover they knew what he had done, especially if he wasn't working alone and other angels were involved, and it was equally as possible that he could reach the mortal world before he could be apprehended.

Lukas didn't doubt that Amaer knew of Annelie, or that he would target her and Serenity in order to make him and Apollyon suffer for what they had done.

He clenched his fists and glared at the male in the images flowing before him.

He would protect them and keep them safe from harm.

He would not fail in this mission.

CHAPTER 13

Lukas landed hard on the terrace of the apartment in Paris as Apollyon released him, causing Serenity and Annelie to shriek. Apollyon's wings beat heavily against the air and he shot away, up into the dark sky, leaving Serenity staring after him.

"What's going on?" Annelie was on her feet and next to him in a heartbeat, concern flashing across her beautiful face.

"My commander is the man responsible for the crime. Apollyon has gone to give evidence to Heaven's Court and to seek the aid of a hunter." Lukas ushered the two women into the apartment and cast a glance around at the darkness before following them in. "We must remain indoors and stay alert."

"You mean he could come here?" Annelie's deep brown eyes widened.

"It is a possibility." One he didn't like entertaining.

There was no sign of trouble so far but he wasn't going to let his guard down until Apollyon returned. He hoped it was soon. His commander was stronger than he was, older and more powerful, and he feared that he wouldn't be able to stand against him if he came.

It wouldn't stop him from trying though.

He would fight until his last breath to keep Annelie and Serenity safe.

Annelie hung back, remaining close to him as Serenity paced the kitchen, glancing at the window every few seconds. He could feel their fear as it laced the air and breathed deep and evenly until his own fear was gone, purged from him by a need to be strong and a desire to protect them, to be the male they needed him to be, showing no fear as he waited for Apollyon's return.

He placed his hand on Annelie's shoulder and then pulled her into his arms when she glanced at him, her dark eyebrows furrowing. He tucked her against him and breathed her in, using the feel of her in his arms to erase everything he had been through in Hell. He was back with her now, and nothing would part them again.

"I will not let him near you," he murmured against her red hair.

She pressed her hands against his white breastplate and leaned into him.

Lukas smoothed her hair and then stroked her arm, trying to soothe her.

He looked across the kitchen island at Serenity as she stopped pacing and started muttering something.

Power rose in her, ebbing outwards through the room and him, tangling with his own. She was casting some sort of spell and, by the feel of it, it was strong on the protection and defence side of things.

Serenity glanced at him. He thanked her with a smile for being so considerate and keeping them safe in her own way. He wasn't sure how well a spell would hold out against an angel's power, but right now, he would try anything.

An hour trickled past as they lingered in the kitchen, waiting for Apollyon's return.

Serenity murmured words that strengthened the spell she had cast, renewing it, and Annelie moved away from him to put the kettle on, her fear fading as she focused on the small task of making tea.

Outside, the world was peaceful.

Perhaps Apollyon had been wrong about his commander and he wasn't coming for them. Apollyon must have spoken to Heaven's Court by now.

The sensation of Serenity's power in the room weakened despite the fact she was still whispering things to herself and a different feeling replaced it, a darker one that crawled over Lukas's skin and made him tense.

They weren't alone.

"Serenity." He caught Annelie's hand and pulled her away from the kettle, towards the witch.

Serenity wrapped her arms around Annelie and crouched in the corner of the kitchen with her. Both women covered their heads with their hands and Serenity spoke more strange words that charged the air with an electric current that had the hairs on his arms standing on end.

The barrier shimmered like a rainbow.

She was reinforcing it.

Lukas held his palm out towards the barrier and focused his own power there, trying to assist her. Magic had a tendency to draw on the strength of all nearby. He was sure that it would sense him and steal from his power to boost itself and Serenity.

He felt it the moment they connected, her power entwining with his, draining his strength, and held his focus. They had to withstand whatever dark force was coming. The air of malevolence in the night thickened until it pressed down on Lukas.

It was closer.

Was it his commander?

He peered out into the night.

The glass in the doors and windows exploded and he swiftly raised his arm to protect his face as shards blasted into him. The women screamed and Lukas reacted on instinct. He barrelled through the broken door and into the person outside, not giving them a chance to attack. They tipped over the railings, hit the small sloping section of lead roof the other side, rolled off it and plummeted towards the ground.

Lukas twisted and turned with his attacker, gaining enough space to see who it was.

Amaer.

The older greying man glared at him, spread his large white wings and gained the upper hand, twisting Lukas beneath him.

He grunted as Amaer grabbed his white breastplate and beat his wings, driving them faster downward, and fought the male, clutching his commander's white vambraces that encircled his forearms and then the straps of his body armour. He tried to turn with him again, so he was on top, but Amaer had the advantage of being able to use his wings.

Lukas wasn't acquitted of his crime yet.

Until he was, he couldn't fly.

The ground came at him fast.

Lukas bellowed when he hit it back first, fracturing the pavement, his commander on top of him. Amaer hit him hard in the gut with his feet, knocking the remaining air from him, and Lukas had to fight to remain conscious.

His vision wavered and when it came back, Commander Amaer's white and gold boot was coming at his face. He frowned, managed to grab Amaer's leg before it connected and growled as he launched Amaer to his right, into a parked car. The alarm wailed as Lukas flipped onto his feet and lunged towards Amaer.

Amaer beat his broad white wings and shot upwards. Lukas pressed down hard with his right foot and leaped, caught his ankle, and yanked, dragging him back down again and ignoring the pain that tore through him as he moved.

He wasn't going to let the man go after Annelie and Serenity.

If it came down to it, he would break the rules and fly. He would do anything to protect them.

Lukas caught Amaer's other leg, swung and smashed him into the hood of the car.

The alarm died and Lukas spun and slammed Amaer into the low wall that surrounded one of the buildings, splintering the stones and knocking several loose.

Amaer gave a vicious snarl, managed to break one leg free and kicked him square in the jaw, knocking his head back and sending his mind spinning. The male was on him before Lukas could stop him. One swift punch followed another, sending Lukas's senses reeling, and he struggled to keep going. He stumbled backwards into the road, towards the cars lining it near the park, trying to block the attacks and find an opening.

He wouldn't give up.

He managed to defend against the next punch, grasped his commander's fist, and twisted it, causing his arm to bend with it and tearing a howl from him. Lukas clenched his teeth and kept turning.

Amaer's wings battered him, striking him hard and knocking him away, and he growled in frustration as the male slipped from his grasp. He tried to catch hold of him again but couldn't make it past his wings, kept being driven back every time he made a grab for him.

He needed to reach him, had to get hold of him again or do something to take this advantage away from his opponent.

An idea came to him.

It was a dirty tactic but right now he didn't care.

Lukas fumbled, making several lunges without success before he finally managed to grab the longest feathers of Amaer's wings. He gave them a sharp tug and Amaer's cry split the night. Lukas pulled harder, until the metre-long feathers came away. He tossed them aside as his plan worked and Amaer put his wings away to protect them.

Amaer turned on him, darkness reigning in his eyes as they swirled with gold fire, and Lukas hurled himself at him, growled as he tackled him and took him down, landing hard with him on the road.

Lukas straddled his chest and slammed his fist into the male's face, knocking his head to one side, and struck him again, so it rolled back again. He grunted as he dealt blow after blow, fuelled by the suffering he had endured the past three years.

Amaer had to pay.

Vengeance against their own kind went against everything that angels stood for but right now Lukas wasn't one of them.

He was an outcast, a sinner, and it was all because of this man.

Blood ran down Amaer's cheeks, his lip split and pouring, teeth bloodied as he bared them and tried to fight him. Lukas clenched his jaw and kept going, filled with a dark need to defeat this male, so blinded by it that he didn't see the fist that hit him or the car he smashed into.

Pain blazed in every bone and burned in his muscles as he clawed his way out of the impact crater he had made in the metal. He groaned as he hit the asphalt, spat blood on it and swayed as he tried to push onto his knees.

Amaer snarled, grasped him by his throat and hauled him onto his feet, shoved him against the battered vehicle and hit him hard. Dark eyes full of fury held Lukas's gaze as he tried to find the strength to fight back. Lukas grunted with each strike, each one that bruised and bloodied his face, and managed to get his hands on the male. He clawed at Amaer, shoved him in the face and gained enough space to knee him in the stomach.

Amaer tripped backward, glared at him and lunged forwards.

And froze.

Slowly turned his head to his right.

It hit Lukas that they weren't alone.

Annelie stood in the middle of the road, the hem of her pale dress fluttering in the night breeze. She stared at them both, her eyes full of horror and fear.

Why had she come down?

Lukas cursed her and then took it back. If she had come down because she had seen him fall, because she had been worried about him, then he couldn't curse her. He could only thank her for showing such love and concern towards him, and do his best to protect her during the fight she had walked into.

He wouldn't let Amaer near her.

He wouldn't allow another innocent human to die, especially one he loved with all of his heart.

He broke towards her, sprinting as fast as he could.

Amaer shot in her direction and Lukas fought to reach her first.

He didn't stand a chance as Amaer unleashed his wings and beat them, easily outstripping him.

Annelie backed off a step and turned to run, but Amaer hit her hard and sent her flying. Lukas's heart stopped as she screamed, as he watched her sail through the air and hit the wall of the apartment building. She landed in a heap on the pavement.

Fury bolted through Lukas, rage so hot his blood boiled and he let out a dark snarl as he launched at Amaer, his focus split between his commander and Annelie.

Her heart pounded fast in his ears and he could feel her pain, but she was conscious at least and he had to take that as a good sign.

Lukas moved around to block Amaer's path to her, giving her a chance to recover and get away. He threw a left hook at Amaer. The male dodged it and struck him hard, ploughing his fist into Lukas's gut and knocking the wind from him. Lukas sucked in a breath and threw himself at Amaer.

As he hit the ground with him, he sensed Annelie move.

He kept his commander pinned beneath him, punching him hard, knocking his head side to side, and hoped that she would make it to safety before Amaer managed to throw him.

It happened sooner than Lukas expected. Amaer pressed his hands to Lukas's white breastplate and blasted him with enough power to send him flying upwards.

Lukas spun in the air, the world twirling around him, and didn't have a chance to right himself before the ground was rushing towards him. He didn't hit it. The moment he was within striking distance, Amaer's foot connected with his chest and sent him shooting sideways, speeding towards a car. His breath left him when he hit it, the metal crumpling beneath the blow and glass exploding across the road.

Darkness loomed, his vision tunnelling, and he struggled to shake it off.

Amaer stumbled a few steps and spread his wings.

Lukas blearily looked up at the roof of the building as he tried to tamp down the pain blazing through him and then at the spot where Annelie had been. She had escaped the scene of the fight but Amaer was going after her. His heart pounded at the thought of her in danger, at the images of what Amaer might do to her and Serenity, sending pain pulsing through every limb.

He couldn't let it happen.

He dropped to his feet and staggered forwards until he was running at his commander.

He wasn't fast enough.

Amaer grinned, his face a mess of cuts, and flew out of reach.

Giving Lukas no choice.

He unfurled his white wings and beat them, ready to fly.

A bright light spiralled downwards and around his commander, freezing him in mid-air with his wings outstretched.

What was happening?

Lukas stumbled to a halt and lifted his hand, using it to shield his eyes from the piercing shaft of light, careful to avoid touching it. His gaze followed it upwards. It speared the night sky, reaching Heaven itself.

A bolt of bright blue shot down the column holding Amaer and his commander bellowed.

Amaer's wings shattered, raining blood and feathers down onto the cars below.

The light flickered and died, and Amaer dropped to the ground, landing face first in the mess of blood and broken feathers.

Lukas breathed hard, fighting the pain filling him, and stared at Amaer. Heaven had banished him. It had judged Amaer and taken his wings completely. The first step in making an angel mortal. It would take his powers next.

Amaer pushed himself onto his knees and glared at Lukas with dark malevolence in his eyes. He held his hand out and cold fear flashed through Lukas when a spear appeared in his grasp.

No.

Amaer stumbled onto his feet and limped towards the entrance to the building.

Lukas gave chase, intent on protecting Annelie and Serenity, but a wave of power surged through him, freezing him to the spot. Pain chased the power, stealing his senses and sending his mind reeling for a second before everything came back online, only he felt different.

Powerful.

He had never realised just how strong he was.

With his powers returned to him by Heaven's Court, a sign of their forgiveness, and the thought of Annelie in danger, he felt invincible. Nothing was going to stand between him and stopping Amaer.

Lukas beat his wings and flew at him. He held both of his hands out in front of him, his index fingers and thumbs against each other, and drew them apart. A white spear accented with gold detailing materialised between his hands and he grabbed it when it was fully realised. He focused on his target and felt the silent command issued to him.

He would obey, but not because Heaven had ordered him. He would do it because he couldn't allow Amaer to harm Annelie and Serenity. He would do it to protect them.

"Amaer!" Lukas held the spear out at his side, the pointed golden blade of it directed at his commander's back.

Amaer stopped in his tracks and slowly turned to face him, bringing his own spear around to defend himself. His dark eyes widened when Lukas drove his white spear through his gut and thrust it forwards, sending him into the wall of the building. It shuddered and a shockwave blasted outwards it as the blade penetrated the bricks, knocking Lukas back into the road.

He stumbled, rolled heels over head and landed on his knees, struggling for breath.

Amaer's spear fell from his hand and clattered to the ground at his feet where they dangled a foot off the pavement. He grabbed Lukas's spear where it punctured his body and cried out as he tried to remove it.

Bright white light descended again, engulfing Amaer. Lukas flinched away, aware of what was coming. Life as a mortal was too good for one who had help take so many human lives. Amaer screamed as he disintegrated, leaving only Lukas's bloodied spear jutting out of the wall.

He stared at it, ears ringing and body aching as he sank back on his heels.

It was over.

CHAPTER 14

Wind gusted against Lukas and he squinted as it blew dust at him, shielded himself with his wings and then came out from behind them when the breeze settled and he sensed the presence of two more angels.

"You did well." Apollyon walked towards him, his long black hair tousled from flying.

A tawny winged angel stood behind him, broad built and glowering. Darkness itself seemed to cling to him, shadowing his features.

Einar.

Lukas was glad to see him again. It had been too long.

Apollyon pulled Lukas onto his feet and nodded skyward. "Heaven's Court offers you an apology and they have rescinded their punishment, cleared your name, and reinstated you to your old position."

The spiral of light began to fade and rise upwards. Lukas's gaze followed it again. He was forgiven. Free. It was what he had always wanted but he didn't feel at all as he had expected.

He looked at the balcony of the apartment high above him.

Annelie and Serenity stood there, leaning over and looking down at him. He couldn't go back to his old life because these past three years had changed him.

He had fallen in love.

Lukas met Apollyon's gaze.

"It is possible to balance life and work... although women will do their best to make it impossible." Apollyon grinned and stared up at the balcony.

"You will reach a decision in time. Do not be hasty to cast aside all that you have worked for. They will only spend months convincing you to stay, making you jump through hoops and wade through red tape, and then they will replace you with a temp and you will end up with twice the workload."

Lukas smiled at the grim look on Apollyon's face. His friend was right. He couldn't be hasty about leaving his duty behind, not when he had thought of nothing but returning and clearing his name.

Einar stepped forwards, cast his dark gaze around the area, and then fixed it on Lukas. He was as distant as always, viewing everything with a critical and clinical eye that suited his position. His tawny armour matched his short ponytail and wings that were flecked with paler hues of brown and grey, marking him as one of the hunter legions.

"Heaven's Court assigned you the best. Einar is their foremost hunter now," Apollyon said with a teasing smile and something told him that Apollyon had lobbied for Einar, not only because he was their best hunter but because he wanted to tell the male about Rook and Isadora.

Apollyon wanted to help them both.

Lukas would be right there with him.

Einar raised his hand. Light emanated from his palm in bright shafts and Lukas could only stare as the cracks in the pavement and walls repaired themselves and the damage to the cars reversed until they were pristine again.

Lukas's knees weakened when the light touched him and he stared at his arms as the cuts and scratches shrank and disappeared, until not even a trace of blood remained.

He had forgotten how powerful Einar was.

"Let us discuss things in more comfortable surroundings." Einar's deep voice echoed in the night and he glanced around the street. "Somewhere less exposed."

Lukas nodded, stretched his wings and smiled as he focused on them. He took a long breath and beat his wings, slowly at first, building up the courage to fly again.

How would Annelie react now that he could do such things? Would she fear him again?

There was only one way of finding out.

He flapped his white wings harder and carefully ascended the height of the building, making sure that he didn't clip the walls. Annelie was waiting for him at the top, holding her left arm, and a smile blossomed on her face when her eyes fell on him. He rose higher, enjoying the feel of the warm air in his feathers, and then descended towards her.

"I was so worried about you. I shouldn't have come down... but I couldn't let you fight alone." She held her right hand out to him, a flicker of fear and guilt in her eyes, and relief swept through him when he realised that she wasn't going to run away now that he was a true angel again.

Lukas landed close to her and gathered her into his arms, wrapping her in his wings to fully protect her and satisfy his desire to know that she was safe. "Are you hurt?"

He pulled back to look at her. She shook her head, but tears shone in her eyes. He cleared a smudge of dirt from her damp cheek and sighed.

"I can feel your pain." Lukas looked her over and frowned when he noticed that her left arm was bleeding.

He carefully took hold of it, cradling it in his hands. Her elbow was cut and already bruising. A cursory glance at her shoulder revealed that it too was scraped and bloodied.

Lukas looked to Einar as he flew down towards them.

The large tawny angel glanced at Annelie and then nodded.

Apollyon set down close to Lukas and Serenity threw her arms around his neck, muttering things in French. He wrapped his arms around Serenity and pulled her close to him, lifting her and pressing a kiss to her shoulder. Her feet barely reached Apollyon's shins as he held her aloft and fussed over her.

Lukas released Annelie and stepped back to make room for Einar.

He landed silently on the black railing around the balcony.

Annelie gasped when Einar held his hand out and white light danced in a wave over her skin. Lukas remained close to her, there for her so she would feel safe. When the light faded, she looked herself over with wide incredulous eyes, and then met his gaze.

She smiled and turned to Einar. "Thank you."

Both women stared at him.

Apollyon covered Serenity's eyes and she giggled, the sound light in the darkness.

"Jealous," she whispered and looped her arm around Apollyon's.

He released her eyes and smiled into them.

Lukas had expected him to deny the emotion she had pinpointed, but he gave her a guilty-as-charged look.

Annelie remained tucked close to Lukas and he was glad of it. He wasn't the type for jealous fits but he was likely to join Apollyon if she even looked at Einar in the wrong way. Einar was strong, undeniably handsome, and the quicker he was gone the happier Lukas would be.

Perhaps he was already jealous.

"The evidence given to the court is troubling. I have alerted the Watchers and a team has been sent to the bottomless pit to evaluate the history recorded there. We will discover the conspiracy and the whereabouts of the demons and I will handle them alone..." Einar remained on the balcony railing, his wings tightly furled against his back, and the hard edge to his expression softened a little, a flicker of warmth entering his eyes as he looked between Lukas and Apollyon. "But if I should require assistance, I will call on you. As always, you have proven yourselves strong."

Einar nodded, released his wings and tipped backwards. He dropped off the edge of the roof, reappeared with a beat of his wings, and was gone again in a gust of wind. Annelie burrowed into Lukas's side as it blew against them and he held her closer as he watched Einar speeding into the night.

"Never was a very talkative fellow." Apollyon sounded amused.

Lukas glanced at him.

He looked it too.

"And who is he to say I have proven myself strong? I thought that was an undeniable fact." Apollyon glared in the direction Einar had flown. "I was casting the Devil into the pit before he was a fledgling."

Lukas smiled. If there was one sure way to irritate Apollyon, it was to undermine his strength and power. Apollyon was likely to release the Devil early and fight him again just to prove how powerful he was. He huffed and Serenity pulled a face of mock-pity.

"I still think you are strong, mon ange." Serenity stroked his arm.

"I could still prove it." Apollyon swept her up and kissed her.

Lukas looked away to find Annelie smiling at them. He pulled her back to him, so her body was flush against his, and stroked the long strands of red hair from her face. She did look stunning in the small pale dress. Good enough to eat.

"I am sorry that I worried you." He brushed the backs of his fingers down her cheek and quietly thanked Apollyon when he sensed him lead Serenity into the apartment, leaving them alone.

"I didn't like seeing you fighting that man." Annelie pressed her hands against the breastplate of his white armour and he wished that her hands were on his skin, warm and soft, slowly traversing his bare body. "Is it over now, like that other angel said?"

Lukas nodded. "Einar will hunt the demons involved. We have uncovered some sort of plot. The people in the factory that blew up were already dead. Einar must discover what happened and why. I want to assist him but it is not my place to investigate such matters. I am more of a mediator and intervention specialist."

"It sounds far less dangerous." There was a smile in her brown eyes and he could feel her relief. "I don't like the thought of you being in danger again..."

She hesitated and looked away from him, her feelings shifting course to ones he couldn't understand. She stared into the distance, in the direction Einar had flown, and tears lined her lashes. What had caused the sudden change in her emotions? What was she thinking to make her look so sad?

Lukas stepped around her, into the path of her gaze, and cupped her cheek. She sniffed and blinked, sending a tear down her cheek. He ached to see it and wiped it away with his thumb.

"Does it still hurt?" He cast a glance at her elbow and shoulder.

"It's not that." She rubbed her eyes and sniffed again. Her gaze darted to his and then back to his chest. Her fingers traced the gold edging of his breastplate. She took a deep breath and looked up into his eyes. "Are you going back to Heaven?"

A smile burst onto his lips and he dragged her close, wrapping his arms tightly around her. He pressed his lips to her forehead and closed his eyes. Foolish woman. As if he was going to leave her now that he had her. She was still the only good thing in his world and he couldn't return to one where she didn't exist.

He kissed her forehead and sighed against it. "I have not yet decided whether to give up my position and live as Apollyon does, but either way I am not going to leave you. I have something in this world my heart desires to protect and that is my mission now. You are more important to me than my duty. I love you, Annelie."

Annelie pulled back, her eyes wide and no longer filled with tears, and kissed him. Her lips danced slowly over his, gradually turning more passionate, and he groaned when she tilted her head and fused their mouths together.

He lifted her and closed his eyes, wishing they were somewhere more private so he could prove to her that he wasn't going anywhere and that he loved her more than anything.

He was free now, his innocence proven, and he wasn't about to rush back into his old life. Apollyon was right. Lukas was going to give his new one his all and see where it took him. Whatever decision he and Annelie made, they would make it together, and he was sure that it would be the right one.

Whether they lived a mortal life or lived forever, he would never stop loving Annelie.

She broke away, her smile wide and beautiful. Her brown eyes met his and a small frown creased her brow.

"Can we see Paris now?" There was mischief in her eyes that said he wasn't the only one thinking of proving their love to the other and wishing they were somewhere a little more private.

"As my love wishes." Lukas swept her up into his arms, holding her close to his chest, and beat his wings, lifting off from the terrace.

Annelie squeaked, wrapped her arms around his neck and curled up. "I wasn't quite thinking this way."

Lukas laughed and flew with her, keeping his grip on her tight. "You are safe, Annelie. I will never let you go now that I have you... and this is the best way to see a city."

Paris spread out before them, lights twinkling in the darkness, but it was incomparable to Annelie's beauty. She came out from her hiding place against his chest, her eyes wide and lips parted as she took everything in. She was breathtaking when she was happy, her love flowing through him, merging with his own feelings, bringing out his smile again.

"Incredible." Her gaze roamed to him and he swooped down, heading for the Arc de Triomphe.

When they had been there to meet Apollyon, he had sensed her desire to remain and take in the view of the city. At the time, he hadn't been able to give her what she wished for but he could now that he was free. He would pander to her every whim, indulge her desires, and never tire of loving her.

He landed quietly on the thick wall of the empty roof of the arch and held Annelie close to him.

"Can we stay here a while?" she whispered, her eyes on the city.

Lukas curled his wings around her and nodded. "For as long as you like."

She sighed and settled her head against his chest. He turned sideways, so she could still see the city, but she moved back and placed her arms around his neck. He looked down into her eyes and blinked slowly.

"If it will not cause a problem with the pub, we can stay in Paris for a while and be together." He pressed a kiss to the tip of her nose and she smiled. "Apollyon has something he and Serenity are working on and I would like to help them."

"That sounds good... but... I want to be together for longer than a while." Annelie stroked his cheek, threaded her fingers into his hair, and teased his earlobe with her thumb. Her dark gaze held his. She hesitated and he knew there was something that she wanted to say, something that she feared to a degree. He held her closer, wanting to comfort her and give her the strength to speak what was on her mind. "Serenity told me all sorts of things."

"She did?" he said to encourage her.

"She said there was a trial that she was going to undertake to become immortal like Apollyon."

Lukas's heart beat faster, hard against his chest. The warm affectionate look in Annelie's eyes said everything that she couldn't. She was considering taking the trial too. He had spent hours trying to think of how to broach the subject of their future and she had done it instead. It relieved him, giving him hope that she wanted to be with him forever and that he might not have to surrender his immortality.

Annelie stroked his wings, tickling his white feathers, and he closed his eyes and rested his forehead against hers.

"It is dangerous." He savoured the feel of her in his arms and her hands on him, not wanting to think about what was ahead of them in the future and focusing on the present instead.

"I don't want you to give up what you've worked so hard for. You fought to make them see your innocence and to win back your wings, and Serenity said that even when Apollyon says that he would sacrifice them for her, she can tell that he would miss them. Angels love to fly apparently."

"We do." Lukas drew back and looked deep into her eyes. "But not as much as I love you. I would give them up if you asked me to."

"I'm not going to ask you to do such a thing. I love you and I want to be with you as you are, as the man I fell for... the angel I fell for." Her fingers caressed his brow and then his cheek, trailing down to his jaw and resting there as her eyes searched his. "When Serenity told me that you might give up your wings, I made my decision. I'm going to do it someday. I'm going to do it so we can be together."

Lukas dropped his head and kissed her, touched by her sincerity and the depth of her desire to be with him. She would go through hell in order to achieve immortality, but there was so much resolve in her eyes and in her words that he knew she wouldn't falter. She would do that for him and he loved her all the more for it, for showing him how strong her feelings for him were and the lengths she was willing to go to in order for them to be together.

When the time came, he would help her through the trials. He would do all he could to support her.

He would love her forever, with all of his heart, because she was the only woman in the world for him, the one who had given him strength when he had been weak, had given him love when all others had forsaken him, and who had believed in him.

For now, he was happy with her like this, in his arms where she belonged.

But one day they would take the next step.

And they would have their forever after.

The End

Read on for a preview of the next book in the Her Angel: Bound Warriors Series, Warrior Angel!

WARRIOR ANGEL

She was heading for trouble.

Einar watched the raven-haired woman walking straight towards a male coming the opposite way through the moonlit park. He beat his tawny wings, keeping his position high above them in the cool air.

The woman appeared and disappeared as she passed under the intermittent streetlamps that lined the paths that snaked through the London park like veins, arteries that had grown quiet over the past hour as night had tightened its hold on the city. The lights used in an attempt to offer guidance and safety through the enormous area of green weren't strong enough to cut through the darkness, leaving the park as a black hole in a sea of glittering golden and white pinpricks.

London stretched as far as he could see in all directions, a golden halo capping it that drowned out the stars and revealed the shadowy shapes of the high-rises and landmarks to him.

Einar swooped lower in the night, wanting to get a better look at the two people and unable to ignore the pressing need to be closer in case he was right and the man wasn't a man at all.

If the demon showed any sign of attacking the woman, he would intervene. Until that happened, he would watch, hidden from them both by his power.

It wasn't his place to interfere in things.

He was here to hunt, not protect.

The steady rush of wind over him chilled his skin, drawing his focus to the world around him again, even as he tried to keep it pinned on the female and the potential demon below him.

Summer was on its way out and autumn was encroaching as surely as the night. The days were growing short and he still hadn't found his demon targets, despite scouring the city for them, chasing every lead he had and every new one he discovered.

Heaven's Court were becoming restless with the desire to know why a commander of theirs called Amaer had sided with three demons, assisting them in the disposal of over one hundred human bodies, and had incriminated a fellow angel, setting him up to take the fall.

Lukas hadn't deserved to have such a thing happen to him. For as long as Einar had known him, the mediator had been one of the most upstanding and loyal angels in Heaven. If Einar had known about his plight earlier, if his old comrade had told him what had happened and how he had been blamed for a crime he hadn't committed, he would have tried to help him sooner.

He had failed to help him clear his name and prove his innocence, but he wouldn't fail to find out what Amaer had been doing and he wouldn't fail to track down the demons who had been involved.

Although, Lukas could have helped him by keeping Amaer alive so Einar could question him. He sighed at that and shook his head. He couldn't blame Lukas. The male had been given an order, and he had fulfilled it, and Heaven hadn't exactly taken a back seat in proceedings. They had been the ones to obliterate Amaer.

Destroying any leads and information Amaer could have given him in the process.

Now his only lead were the demons.

Einar sensed the woman moving closer and his focus snapped back to her.

She was close to the man now.

Einar's hand went to the hilt of the blade hanging from his waist. The vambrace protecting his forearm was cold against the strip of stomach exposed between his rich brown and gold breastplate and the pointed strips of armour that protected his hips.

It wouldn't be long before he had to wear winter armour, which meant this hunt was taking too long. It was wearing him down now. He couldn't remember the last time he had slept for more than a few hours before waking, driven by a restlessness that demanded he keep searching for the demons and answers.

It was beginning to affect his concentration.

A noise from below snagged his attention. He silently cursed himself as the woman reared back as the man lunged for her, her black hair dancing in the breeze as she attempted to evade him.

Einar beat his wings and shot towards her.

Slammed to a halt in mid-air barely a few metres above her, unable to believe his eyes as she drew a short silver blade from beneath the back of her black jacket and started to fight.

She was breathtaking.

He could only stare as she fought the male demon who still wore his human form.

Her movements were fluid, mesmerising, made only more graceful by her slender figure and the tight clothes that hugged her long legs, trim waist and lean torso. She swung her right leg around, connecting hard with the demon's head, and the male grunted and snarled as he struggled to shake off the blow. The moment her foot touched the floor, she brought it back again, catching the demon unawares and unguarded.

He toppled sideways, losing balance and fighting to remain upright.

She kicked off on a low grunt, barrelling towards the demon and putting him on the back foot, keeping him off balance with lunges and swipes of the short blade.

It gleamed brightly in the moonlight, flashes of white and silver lines marking its deadly path.

Einar beat his wings to keep steady, bewitched by the woman and her ability to fight, unable to bring himself to move despite the need to help her that steadily built inside him.

He couldn't stop himself from admiring her, didn't want to disturb her or make her aware of him, because he feared it would end the alluring dance she was performing with her opponent.

He had never thought a female could have such skill.

He had only ever met females that needed tending to and protecting.

This one was different. She handled a weapon with ease, and with skill almost matching his own, and she radiated confidence and strength that said she could take care of herself. It didn't stop him from wanting to intervene in her fight, but he was damned if he could convince himself to move.

The male demon snarled and shifted his shoulders. Black ragged scaly wings erupted from his back, tearing through his dark shirt, and his hands became talons.

Einar's eyes narrowed.

The history recorded in the pool in Hell had revealed the type of demon that had committed the sin of killing the innocent humans.

This man was one of their breed.

Einar's dark gaze leaped to the woman, because he was sure she would be horrified, shocked or possibly even already fleeing, and he refused to let the demon get the jump on her, was ready to swoop down and assist her, taking over the battle against the male.

She didn't even hesitate at the sight of the man's wings and claws. She continued her attack, evading every lunge and swipe he made at her, dealing blows of her own in return whenever she could get close enough and showing no sign of running.

If anything, she was putting more effort into the fight now that the demon had revealed himself.

Which meant she wasn't a stranger to this sort of creature.

The demon screeched and launched himself at her, still half in his human guise.

She blocked each slash of his talons with her short sword but the demon was forcing her backwards now, putting her off balance this time. She rallied, kicking the demon in the shin and then aiming another one at his chest.

Time seemed to slow as the demon grinned, easily caught her ankle and twisted, hurling her along the pavement. She tumbled, arms and legs flailing, her weapon flying across the grass, and stopped a few metres away from the demon. She was still for a moment, a heartbeat that seemed like an eternity to Einar as he focused on her, needing to see if she was hurt or worse, unconscious and vulnerable, and then she growled a dark curse.

Her long dark hair covered her face as she struggled to get to her feet.

Cold fury curled through Einar's veins, tightening his muscles. He flexed his fingers around the hilt of his sword and gripped it so tightly his bones hurt.

He had seen enough.

The demon ran at the woman.

Einar swept down between them, dropping the glamour that concealed him from their eyes at the same time as he drew his sword, and blocked the demon's attack.

The male snarled and hissed through his fangs as he leaped backwards, placing some distance between them.

Einar pulled down a deep breath, steadying himself as he waited, holding the demon's dark gaze as the male stared at him, his expression constantly shifting as he studied Einar.

Was he thinking of running?

He wouldn't get far.

If he was thinking of attacking him, he would meet the same fate.

If he was thinking about reaching the woman to hurt her?

Einar needed the male alive, but he would kill the wretch if he had to in order to protect her.

He stretched his tawny wings out to shield her where she struggled behind him. The rich smell of her blood filled the air as she muttered black things under her breath. The demon would pay for hurting her, after he had extracted information from him.

The urge to glance over his shoulder to check on her was powerful, consuming, but he denied it, keeping his focus on the demon instead. He would tend to her once he had dealt with the demon.

The male twitched.

Einar readied himself.

"Get out of my damn way, you big oaf," the woman bit out just as the demon charged them.

Einar turned towards her. Was she speaking to him?

She crouched, tugged the right leg of her dark jeans up, revealing her black leather boot, and the next thing Einar knew, she had a knife in her hand and was running past him.

Resilient, resourceful, but foolish.

Unless she wanted to get herself killed.

She lunged at the demon on a battle cry that stirred Einar's blood in a way he really didn't want to examine.

The demon lashed out, slamming the back of his right hand into the side of her head, sending her skidding across the dewy grass. She landed in a heap and didn't move this time.

Einar beat his tawny wings and shot towards the demon, his blade aimed directly at the male. The demon barely had a chance to look at him before Einar's sword was through his gut, ripping a bellow from him. Einar locked gazes with the demon, clenched his jaw and twisted the sword, tearing another pained cry from him.

"Tell me where the others are hiding," Einar growled and the flicker of fear in the demon's eyes told him everything he needed to know. He was right. This demon was one of them. "Tell me, and you will live. Do not tell me, and I will banish you to Hell to face your master instead."

The demon's eyes widened and he shook his head.

He opened his mouth.

Strange cold rushed from below Einar's feet.

Before he could move, a column of darkness swept up and around them, engulfing both him and the demon. Intense heat and a vivid golden glow lit the ground beneath them as the column rapidly expanded and he tightened his grip on the demon as he felt power pushing at him.

He couldn't lose the male, couldn't lose the information he could give him, the lead he so desperately needed and felt sure this demon was about to offer him.

His boots lifted off the floor.

His grip slipped.

Einar bit out an oath as a blast of the dark power flung him backwards, sending him tumbling heels over head into the sky. He stretched his wings out, gritted his teeth as they caught the currents and twisted painfully, and grinned as he managed to beat them, stopping his ascent.

He turned and plummeted back towards the demon.

A bright flash blinded him and he instinctively shielded his eyes.

When the light dissipated, he lowered his hand and stared down at where the demon had been.

A charred circle on the ground was all that remained, together with the sickening stench of brimstone hanging in the cool night air.

A dark curse rolled off Einar's tongue as he landed gently, sheathed his sword, and walked to the burnt patch of path. He crouched beside it, reached out and hovered his hand over the warm ashes. A sigh lifted his shoulders, causing his breastplate to shift.

Had someone done this to stop the demon from talking?

It wasn't the Devil. He took no interest in such affairs and Einar's threat had been just that—a threat. The Devil wouldn't do anything if Einar could banish a demon to Hell to face the consequences. If anything, he would probably congratulate the demon for doing something to annoy Heaven and the angels.

A groan from the darkness snapped Einar out of his thoughts.

The woman.

He twisted towards her.

She pressed her hands into the grass, her arms shaking as she tried to push herself up. Her tangled fall of dark hair swayed as she struggled, concealing her face from him but not her voice. She was still muttering obscenities, had a tongue a demon would be proud of as she managed to get onto her feet.

The smell of blood grew stronger.

She touched her arm, brought her hand out in front of her, and promptly collapsed.

WARRIOR ANGEL

A powerful hunter angel, Einar is on a mission to discover why one of his kind was working with demons, but it isn't going well... until he finds one of the demons stalking a beautiful woman. When the male attacks, Einar can't stop himself from saving her, even when he knows Heaven will hold it against him—the alluring, lethally seductive woman is half demon.

Taylor vowed long ago to protect her city from the lowest demons and she sure as hell isn't about to let an angel waltz in and take over, and she's definitely not about to fall in love with him, even if he is gorgeous. Determined to do her job as a hunter, she convinces the dangerously sensual warrior to team up with her, but resisting the attraction that blazes between them soon becomes impossible.

As the mission leads them deep into London's underworld and desire flares white-hot between them, can they stop the flames of their passion from consuming them? And can a love so forbidden ever have a happy ending?

Available in ebook and paperback

ABOUT THE AUTHOR

Felicity Heaton is a New York Times and USA Today best-selling author who writes passionate paranormal romance books. In her books she creates detailed worlds, twisting plots, mind-blowing action, intense emotion and heart-stopping romances with leading men that vary from dark deadly vampires to sexy shape-shifters and wicked werewolves, to sinful angels and hot demons!

If you're a fan of paranormal romance authors Lara Adrian, J R Ward, Sherrilyn Kenyon, Kresley Cole, Gena Showalter, Larissa Ione and Christine Feehan then you will enjoy her books too.

If you love your angels a little dark and wicked, her best-selling Her Angel romance series is for you. If you like strong, powerful, and dark vampires then try the Vampires Realm romance series or any of her stand alone vampire romance books. If you're looking for vampire romances that are sinful, passionate and erotic then try her London Vampires romance series. Or if you like hot-blooded alpha heroes who will let nothing stand in the way of them claiming their destined woman then try her Eternal Mates series. It's packed with sexy heroes in a world populated by elves, vampires, fae, demons, shifters, and more. If sexy Greek gods with incredible powers battling to save our world and their home in the Underworld are more your thing, then be sure to step into the world of Guardians of Hades.

If you have enjoyed this story, please take a moment to contact the author at **author@felicityheaton.com** or to post a review of the book online

Connect with Felicity:
Website – http://www.felicityheaton.com
Blog – http://www.felicityheaton.com/blog/
Twitter – http://twitter.com/felicityheaton
Facebook – http://www.facebook.com/felicityheaton
Goodreads – http://www.goodreads.com/felicityheaton
Mailing List – http://www.felicityheaton.com/newsletter.php

FIND OUT MORE ABOUT HER BOOKS AT:
http://www.felicityheaton.com

Printed in Great Britain
by Amazon

22075345R00081